The Forgeron Legacy

Book One of Alteria

By Jacquelyn D. Atchison

Published by Kadler Publishing

First Published, 2013

Print Edition

Dedication

To my fiancé, Anthony de Leon, for without you this book would have never happened.

Prologue

The night was dark, no moon shone in the cold September sky to provide light to see by. On the outskirts of town, at the end of a long gated driveway a house was in it's final stages of construction. It was a large house, a two-story cottage that the owners had spent months designing. The Wellworths were only waiting for the interior to be painted before moving in. The closest neighbor was half a mile away. There was no one around to see a car pull up to the empty house or two figures creeping up to the door.

"It's locked." Alexandra whispered, tugging on the doorknob. She stared, wide-eyed into the pitch-black darkness of the night. Her ears twitched at the slightest sound, every creak of the porch and rustling of the trees in the mid-autumn breeze. Turning back to the door she rattled the doorknob desperately.

"I'll open it." Ryker replied. Alexandra stepped back and Ryker handed her the box he had been carrying. Placing his hand over the lock, Ryker closed his eyes and focused. Alexandra glanced around nervously, absentmindedly tugging on the drawstring of her hoodie. When she heard the lock click open she looked back, startled. Ryker opened the door and took a step inside, his eyes scanning the dark interior. He held up a hand, motioning for Alexandra to stay outside as he listened intently for any sound in the house. Satisfied that the house was empty he turned and nodded.

"Are you sure about this?" Ryker murmured, taking the box back from Alexandra as she brushed past him. Alexandra turned on a small flashlight she had been carrying in her pocket and crept across the foyer and down the hall into the main part of the house.

"We don't really have another option." She replied. "Come on. The laundry room is this way, the attic will be just above it."

Ryker stood for a moment in the entryway, watching Alexandra as she walked away. With a slight shake of his head he adjusted his grip on the box and followed her.

In the laundry room Alexandra stood under the hatch that lead to the attic and stared up at it, her expression pensive. Ryker stopped beside her and carefully set the box on the floor.

"Is this it?" He asked, indicating the hatch.

Alexandra nodded silently, her gaze never leaving the square piece of wood set into the ceiling. Ryker looked down at her and saw a strain in her features that hadn't been there before. Her usual smiling mouth was pinched tight and tension had creased the skin around her eyes. This last year had aged her, aged them both.

Ryker moved the box to one side with his foot and pulled the hatch down, carefully sliding down the ladder attached to the inside of the door. While he was doing that, Alexandra crouched down next to the box and slipped a journal out of her jacket. Flipping to the last page she grabbed a pen out of her pocket and began writing.

August 12, 1996
This is my last entry. I have seen the outcome of my decisions and I know that this is the only thing I can do in good conscious. It is not easy to leave my daughter, especially knowing that I will never see her again. The decision is even harder knowing the challenges she will be facing. There is so much I wish I could tell her but all I can do is leave this journal and hope that she will find the right path.

Then Alexandra pulled a folded piece of paper from her pocket. She stroked her finger along the edge of the paper, eyes bright with unshed tears. On the inside cover of the journal near the seam there was a small rip in the bottom corner. Carefully pulling up the seam Alexandra slipped the paper in between the seam and the back cover, smoothing the cover back into place when she was done. Only a slight bump betrayed that there was anything there.

Alexandra tucked the journal into the cardboard box with a sigh. Then she picked up a plain wooden box that had been lying next to where she placed the journal in the cardboard box. Alexandra stroked her hand against the smooth top. The glossy finish of the wood shone in the dim lighting.

"You ready?" Ryker asked, once the ladder was secured against the floor.

Opening the box Alexandra slipped off the bracelet she was wearing and placed it inside. She stared at the bracelet, committing every detail of it to memory. Three leather strands braided around each other with smooth metal discs woven into the design. Strange symbols she didn't recognize were etched into the small metal discs. She rubbed her finger across one of them, feeling a pang of regret that she would never find out what they meant. Once again, as she had often felt in the past, Alexandra was amazed that something so simple and ordinary looking could be so important.

Ryker frowned, opening his mouth to say something before changing his mind and pursing his lips together. He watched with narrowed eyes as Alexandra put the bracelet inside the wooden box, then placed it back in the cardboard box. Closing up the cardboard box Alexandra looked up at Ryker and nodded. Ryker knelt next to her and kissed her on the forehead, brushing away the tear that slipped down her cheek with his thumb.

Alexandra gave Ryker a small watery smile. Reaching up she cupped the back of his hand with hers and pressed a soft kiss to the center of his palm. Then she drew in a resolute breath and pushed herself to her feet, stepping away from the box as she wrapped her arms around herself.

Alexandra watched Ryker climb the ladder and disappear up into the attic with the cardboard box. She could hear his footsteps as he crossed to the corner of the attic and the soft sound of the box being placed on the floor. Then Ryker's footsteps returned and she watched as one large foot, then another, appeared on the ladder.

Jumping off the bottom of the ladder Ryker brushed sawdust off himself before folding the ladder back up and closing the attic hatch.

"It's not too late to change your mind." He told her, looking at her with level grey eyes.

Alexandra shook her head. "This is the only way."

"What if you get hurt?" He reached out and brushed his fingers across her cheek.

Alexandra glanced down for a moment before taking his hand in hers. "Come on." She said. "We need to get going."

No one saw the two as they moved stealthily out of the empty house and drove away. When the workers arrived at the house two days later no one noticed the small unmarked box hidden away in the corner of the attic.

CHAPTER ONE

March 12, 2011...

Emma flopped back onto her bed with a groan. She hated mornings. No matter how much sleep she got, and she slept a lot, it never seemed to be enough. As she lay there she mentally recited the reasons she had to get out of bed. Breakfast, school, she'd be late if she didn't wake up and if she showed up late to her first class one more time Mr. Schneider was going to give her detention, so she would be stressed to get there on time and if she was stressed in the morning her whole day would be off.

None of these reasons apparently mattered to her tired body, as it kept trying to lull her mind back to sleep. It was only through a heroic effort on her part that she managed to resist the urge to sleep. Emma cracked open an eyelid and glanced at the clock next to her bed. 7 a.m. About two hours before Emma ever wanted to be awake. What had students ever done to deserve the punishment of school beginning at eight in the morning?

As she watched another minute tick by on the clock Emma realized she was just delaying the inevitable. Mentally saying a sad farewell to the comforting warmth of her bed, Emma slowly sat up and placed her feet on the floor. Sleepily rubbing her eyes she shuffled out of her room and followed the delicious smell of French toast and bacon down the stairs and into the kitchen.

The house she lived in with her adopted family, the Wellworths, was a beautiful country style house with hardwood floors and large windows framed by flower print curtains. Outside, a white picket fence lined the impeccable property. Bright flowerbeds showed off their splashes of color against the white fence across the perfectly trimmed green grass of the yard. Inside, the house was decorated with bright cheerful colors that could have competed with the flowerbeds in the front of the property. There were more flower prints than Emma could handle. As usual everything was spotless and perfect.

Emma stumbled her way to her seat at the table across from Morgan, her entire focus centered on staying awake and upright.

"*Finally.*" Morgan drawled in a long-suffering voice. "Can we eat now, Mom?"

Emma glanced up in time to catch the glare Morgan shot at her. Morgan was already dressed in dark pants and a light brown jacket, her pale blonde hair styled in graceful straight layers and her make-up flawless. Just once Emma wished she could see Morgan looking like a train wreck in the morning.

Emma ignored Morgan's obvious annoyance, choosing instead to focus on the plate of French toast Kathryn was carrying to the table. The ability for speech always seemed to elude Emma before she had had something to eat and on a daily basis it astonished her how many things Kathryn could think of to say before breakfast.

"Good morning, dear!" Kathryn greeted Emma cheerfully as she placed the plate on the table. "Did you sleep well last night?"

If there was ever any question of where Morgan came from all anyone had to do was look at Kathryn. The same pale blonde hair brushed Kathryn's shoulders in a classy, elegant style she had kept for years. The same beautiful features and pale blue eyes showed on both women's faces. But where Morgan was cold Kathryn's eyes glowed with friendly warmth and her mouth was much quicker to smile than to sneer. It was easy to imagine her as the cheerleader she had been in high school and college. Emma never understood why Morgan complained so much about looking like her mother.

Emma managed to nod her head in response to Kathryn's question, quickly grabbing the plate of French toast and snagging two slices before Morgan snatched the plate away from her. Not to be outdone, Morgan grabbed the syrup from the table and slowly drizzled it on her French toast as Emma glared at her, impatiently waiting for her to finish.

"That's great!" Kathryn said, spreading a thin layer of butter on her French toast. She didn't notice Morgan keeping the syrup just out of Emma's reach. "I just love a good night's sleep, especially when I get to wake up to a morning as beautiful as this one. There is nothing quite like waking up to the sound of birds singing and getting to watch the sun rise."

Emma just grunted non-commitally. Morgan had pushed the syrup as far away from Emma as possible and was gloatingly eating her breakfast while Emma just sat there and glared. Morgan smirked at her and for just a moment, a tiny moment, Emma wished she could do something to wipe that smug grin off of Morgan's face.

As soon as the thought popped into her head sharp pain stabbed at her temples, the beginning of one of her headaches. Emma winced and pressed the heel of her palm against her temple, glaring more obviously at Morgan who glared back with equal zeal. Both girls were focused so intently on each other that they didn't notice the syrup beginning to tremble on the table.

"Good morning ladies."

Steve, their dad, walked behind Morgan to his seat at the table, snagging the syrup away from her and handing it to Emma. Emma gave him a grateful smile as he sat down and he winked in return.

"Morgan," He said, directing attention onto her as she hurried to eat her French toast. "Have you gotten any leads on jobs yet?"

At her father's question Morgan's expression turned sour.

"No." She said sullenly. "No one is hiring right now."

"That's not true, dear," Her mother replied. "Mrs. White was just asking our church group last week if we knew anyone who could work in her bookstore part time while she took care of her mother who is about to have surgery. I could tell her you're available."

"A bookstore? No, thanks." Morgan said, wrinkling her nose in distaste. "How lame of a job would that be?"

"I'd like to work there." Emma spoke up. Kathryn looked a little startled to hear Emma speak but she quickly recovered and gave her a big smile.

"Are you sure, dear?" She asked. "It's not going to be very exciting. I'm sure you have other things you'd rather do."

Emma shrugged. "I could use the extra money."

Kathryn smiled. "Alright then, I'll give her a call this afternoon and let her know that you're interested."

"And Morgan, you and I can discuss different employment options for you this afternoon when I get back from the office." Steve said firmly, before standing up and taking his plate to the sink. Morgan made a face at him behind his back, grumbling under her breath about how unfair he was being. Emma stood up from the table and grabbed her plate as well, careful not to make eye contact with Morgan as she walked to the kitchen to put her dishes away. Then she was out of the kitchen and darting up the stairs, not slowing down until she had shut the door behind her.

Emma glanced at the clock on her bedside table. 7:15, displayed in glowing blue numbers. She had fifteen minutes to finish getting ready before she had to leave. Grabbing the first clothes she could find, Emma quickly got dressed and rushed to the bathroom to brush her teeth and drag a brush through her hair.

Looking at her reflection Emma grimaced at how tired she looked. She didn't have a lot of time to do her make-up, so she quickly put on eye liner and mascara, accepting the fact that she would just have to look as tired as she felt that day. As she hurried back into her room Emma glanced at the clock again. 7:28. She had two minutes before she had to leave.

Emma grabbed her backpack off the floor next to her desk and threw it on her bed, stuffing the books that were scattered on the desk into it. Once she had managed to stuff them in with the other books that were already in her bag she wrestled to close the bulging backpack and glanced around the room. She was missing something, she knew it. Deciding it must not be that important, Emma grabbed her backpack and ran out of her room. Two seconds later she ran back in.

"Shoes." She muttered to herself. "Shoes are important."

She found one of the soft brown boots she wanted and sat on her bed to pull it on over her jeans as she searched the room for the other one. It took her a few seconds to remember she had kicked it under the bed at some point. Dropping to her hands and knees, she reached under her bed for the other boot. As she struggled to pull it on she looked at the clock again. 7:31. She was officially running late.

"Great." She muttered, yanking the boot on.

Jumping up, Emma grabbed her backpack from the bed and her favorite necklace from the dresser and ran out of her room for the second time. The house had a three car garage but Morgan had claimed the third car lot as soon as she had turned sixteen a month before Emma, so Emma parked her small two door Toyota Celica next to the house on the gravel. She heard Morgan's garage door open but didn't look up as she dug through the front pocket of her backpack for her keys. Then she heard Morgan's voice behind her.

"Looking for these?" Morgan taunted.

Emma got a sinking feeling in her stomach as she turned around to see Morgan dangling Emma's keys from her finger.

"Give me my keys Morgan, I don't have time to play any games with you right now." Emma said, holding out her hand. A headache started building right behind her forehead as she watched Morgan's lips curl into a smirk.

"I'm not playing any games," Morgan said innocently. "I just wanted to tell you that I'm not mad at you for making me look bad in front of my parents. You know, by volunteering for that job I didn't want."

Morgan always referred to Kathryn and Steve as "my parents".

"That's great," Emma cut in impatiently, conscious of the time being wasted as Morgan kept her there. "Can I have my keys now?"

"At first I was mad," Morgan continued as if Emma hadn't spoken. "After all, you did it just to make me look bad."

"I did not!" Emma protested, but Morgan raised a hand to silence her.

"Then I thought about it and I realized it is a great idea for you to get a job because that will be more time for you to be somewhere else and not around me." Morgan said with a sneer.

"I'm glad I could help." Emma replied drily. She didn't have time for Morgan's dramatics right now. "Now will you give me my keys, please?"

Morgan playfully dangled the keys just out of Emma's reach. "Aren't you going to get in trouble if you're late to class?" She asked sweetly. "I heard Mr. Schneider say he was going to give you detention if you were tardy again today. Little Emma Rose, spending another Saturday in detention."

The dull ache was now a full-blown pain in her head. Emma rubbed her forehead and narrowed her eyes against the stabbing pain. Before she had a chance to reply Kathryn poked her head out of the garage.

"Girls? What are you still doing here? You're going to be late!" She exclaimed, flapping her hands in a shooing gesture.

"I was just giving Emma her keys," Morgan replied, "She forgot them on the entryway table."

Morgan held the keys out to Emma but just as Emma went to reach for them Morgan dropped them. Emma's hand snaked through the air but just as she was about to grasp the keys a large shadow flitted into the corner of her vision and she flinched away. The keys fell to the ground in a rattling heap. Morgan snorted in amusement.

"Freak." She said, tossing her hair over her shoulder as she walked to her car.

Emma glanced to the side where she had seen the shadow but nothing was there. Regaining her composure Emma stuck her tongue out at Morgan's back. It was childish but it made her feel a little better. Scooping her keys off the ground Emma ran to her car and jumped in. 7:40. Emma groaned as she shifted her car into reverse and pulled out of the driveway. She was going to be late to class. She hoped Mr. Schneider was in a good mood today.

‘

‘

CHAPTER TWO

The normally jam-packed hallways of Riverdale High were empty of students. Teacher's voices were a quiet murmur behind the closed doors of the classrooms, not nearly loud enough to cover the noise of Emma's feet slapping against the linoleum as she ran. Emma was almost there, her classroom was just around the corner at the end of the hallway. Blue lockers flashed by as she sprinted as fast as she dared and skidded around the corner. Too late, did she notice a guy standing in the middle of the hallway.

Emma tried to stop her mad dash but her shoes had little traction on the slick linoleum floor. The soft soles of her boots slid her across the floor straight towards the guy, slamming her directly into his chest. Emma felt like she had hit a brick wall. The impact knocked her backward off her feet sending her into a free fall towards the floor. Emma could only brace herself for the inevitable impact. But it never came. Before she hit the floor the guy caught her by the hand, halting her fall with just an inch to spare.

Emma blinked up at him, as the guy slowly eased her to the floor and she realized that she didn't know him. Even in a school of 2000 students she knew for sure she had never seen him before because guys this good looking didn't exist in Riverdale. She had checked. His dark hair tumbled in slight waves onto his forehead and over his ears as he bent down to look at her with deep blue eyes that stared down into hers with a slightly amused expression. He was fighting a grin, she could tell from the way his lips were twitching but she didn't care. She was too distracted by the hint of a dimple she could see. She bet if he smiled it would turn into a full-fletched heart melting dimple. *I'm in so much trouble.* Emma thought. She blushed when she realized she was still sitting on the floor, holding his hand gazing up at him like an idiot.

"You okay?" He asked, gently pulling her up.

Emma nodded wordlessly, so embarrassed she could hardly bring herself to look him in the eye. His gorgeous, blue eyes. Yep, she was definitely in trouble.

"You certainly pack a hit for a little girl." He smiled ruefully, rubbing his chest with one large hand.

She immediately opened her mouth to argue that she wasn't little, but then she realized that he still towered over her even though she was standing up. Words began tumbling out of her mouth. "I am so sorry! I hope you're okay, I can't believe I ran into you like that! Are you okay?"

He laughed and waved off her concern. "Don't worry, after a season of having a bunch of guys trying to tackle me every day it's nice to have a girl try." He said with a wink.

Emma felt heat rush to her face and realized she must be blushing again. She looked down, nervously tugging her shirt straight. Then his words finally sank in and she blinked in confusion.

"Guys?" She asked, glancing shyly up at him.

"Football." He replied with a smile.

"Ohhh, okay." Emma nodded. That made sense, he was definitely built like an athlete. Emma frowned as she looked at him. "You're not one of our football players, I would have recognized you…Are you?" She asked uncertainly.

"I just transferred here." He told her, shifting his backpack higher on his shoulder. "You're actually the first person I've met. I'm Jason by the way." Jason smiled down at her as he held out a hand, showing off the dimple that she had wondered about.

Emma shook his hand, trying not to look too awestruck. "Nice to meet you, Jason." She whispered. There was a pause as they both looked at each other, neither saying a word. Emma felt like she was missing something. Jason raised his eyebrows slightly, his smile deepening even further.

18

"And your name is…?" He prompted.

Heat rushed to Emma's face all over again. "Emma!" She blurted. "My name is Emma. Wow, I'm normally better at this."

"Better at what?" Jason finally let go of her hand and took a small step back, giving her some space to breath. Emma sucked in a breath, able to think clearly again now that he wasn't so close.

"Being normal." Emma replied depreciatingly, giving a little half smile.

Jason chuckled. "Normal is boring. No one I've ever met who's interesting is normal."

"And if I was interesting I'd be okay with that, but if I'm not normal or interesting then I would just be a boring oddity and who wants to know someone like that?" Emma quipped back.

"I would like to know you, even if you were a boring oddity. But I think you're interesting, so you're safe." Jason replied.

"Thanks." Emma said with a shy smile.

Jason shifted closer to her and opened his mouth to say something else when the door to the class room suddenly swung open and Mr. Schneider stood in the doorway glaring down at Emma.

"Miss Rose, you realize that in order to be counted as present you need to actually be present in the room?" Emma could practically see the icicles hanging from his words as he spoke. Frosty would have been putting it nicely.

"Yes Mr. Schneider, and I apologize." Emma began to explain what had happened when Jason smoothly cut in.

"It's my fault sir," He spoke up, drawing Mr. Schneider's attention away from Emma. "Emma was just helping me since I'm new here."

Mr. Schneider's eyes narrowed as he looked at Jason, clearly skeptical of anything positive about Emma.

"Miss Rose it seems as though for once your tardiness is excusable. However, make sure that you do not teach Mr. Silverstone your poor attendance habits. Please take your seat. Mr. Silverstone, follow me to my desk."

When Mr. Schneider turned and walked back into the room Emma mouthed a quick "Thank you" to Jason before she slipped into the room and went to her seat in the back corner.

Emma didn't remember much of that day's lecture. She was too focused on not looking at Jason but also trying to look at him out of the corner of her eye to see if he was looking at her. Maybe it was because of her intense concentration to not look at Jason but class flew by that day. Before Emma knew it the bell was ringing and everyone was stuffing their books in their backpacks and filing out the door. Emma couldn't remember a single thing Mr. Schneider had talked about during class, she didn't even know what subject they were covering.

As she packed up her stuff she decided to read the assigned chapters in the book that night for the first time that year. If she wasn't going to be listening in class she should probably do the reading. Emma was so lost in her thoughts as she stuffed her books into her backpack that she didn't notice someone standing next to her. A hand dropped on her shoulder, startling her so much that she nearly jumped out of her seat.

"Hey, I didn't mean to startle you." Jason said, smiling down at her. "I was just wondering if you could tell me where D150 is. That's my next class and I have no idea how to get there."

"Of course!" Emma flashed him her best smile, "I'm actually headed that way myself. My next class is on the floor above yours."

"Great, I was hoping you were going in that direction." Jason sounded relieved. For a second Emma let herself hope that he wanted to spend more time with her but then... "I don't know anyone else yet, and I hate wandering around like I don't know what I'm doing."

Emma forced herself to laugh lightly. "Don't worry, you don't have to walk by yourself." So much for him wanting to spend time with her.

Grabbing her backpack she stood up and headed out of the classroom. Jason followed Emma out of the room and into the crowded hallway, sticking close behind her. Students stood at their lockers grabbing books and formed in small groups along the sides of the hall to talk. The students on their way to classes formed two lanes of traffic in the middle of the hallway, one going each direction. Emma pushed her way through the crowd until she got into the line of students moving towards the doors. She glanced over her shoulder to make sure Jason was still behind her.

His eyebrows were lowered over his eyes in a slight frown as he kept glancing back and forth, like he was tracking every movement. He had his shoulders hunched forward as he pushed his way through the crowd after her and every moment in the crowd seemed to heighten his tension. Finally they made it outside and away from the overwhelming crush of students. She watched Jason as he breathed a sigh of relief and relaxed.

"Do you not like crowds?" Emma glanced at him out of the corner of her eye, curious but not wanting to pry.

Jason looked at her quizzically. "What do you mean?"

"You just seemed a little tense back there, that's all." Emma said lightly, looking forward.

They were walking across the quad now, a giant open space in the middle of campus with sidewalks crisscrossing over the lawn heading to different buildings. They were on the sidewalk that headed to the north side of campus where the D building was.

Emma watched as everyone who passed them stared at Jason, the girls in admiration and the guys in annoyance. She couldn't help but smirk when a few of the prettier girls cast openly jealous looks in her direction. There was nothing going on between her and Jason but it was still nice to be the focus of envy for once.

"Crowds can overwhelm me a little bit sometimes." Jason explained. "I'm more of an open spaces type of guy."

"I'm the same way." Emma agreed. "I could never live in a city, too many people around all the time. I love being able to see the sky and open land, to be near nature."

"Yeah, exactly." Jason nodded his head enthusiastically.

"So do you have first lunch or second lunch?" Emma asked. *Please let him have first lunch.*

"I'm not sure, let me check." Jason reached into the side pocket of his backpack and pulled out a piece of paper. "Umm, it says I have Lunch A, so I'm guessing first lunch?"

Emma grinned, a lot happier than she probably should have been to hear that. "Yes, that's first lunch. I think it's the better lunch to have because then lunch divides the classes evenly. I don't think I could make it through four classes before eating lunch."

"Do you have first lunch too?" Jason asked as they left the quad and approached the D building.

"Yeah, my best friend Amy and I made sure we did." Emma said with a smile. She pushed open the door to the D building and the two of them squeezed inside. They paused in a small open space just inside the doors of the building next to the staircase while crowds of students pushed past them.

"Maybe I'll see you at lunch then." Jason said, raising his voice a little to be heard above the crowd.

Emma nodded. "I'll keep an eye out for you."

Just then the warning bell rang, letting all the students know they had one minute to get into their classrooms. Emma waved a quick goodbye to Jason as she ran up the stairs to her next class. She barely managed to get into the room before Mrs. Kelso closed the door.

"Cutting it close today Emma." Mrs. Kelso said teasingly.

"I always do." Emma replied cheekily. She liked Mrs. Kelso. The woman had a great sense of humor and was a good teacher.

As she sat down at her desk Emma took a deep breath, already thinking about what she would do if she saw Jason at lunch.

Emma hurried to the cafeteria, not bothering to stop at her locker and drop off books like she normally did. She joined a long line of students attempting to crowd into the cafeteria from the only inside entrance. Everyone else who had their last class in other buildings poured into the room from the three outside entrances. In just a few minutes there would be no seats left in the room and those unlucky enough not to have one would have to go outside or find someplace else to eat their lunch.

Emma pushed through the crowd and waved to Amy when Emma saw her sitting at their usual table.

"Nice bow." Emma said as she walked up.

Amy's blonde hair was tied back in a high ponytail with a bright red polka dot bow that was perfectly coordinated with her red outfit for the day.

"Thanks!" Amy said, smiling brightly. She scooted over on the bench to make room for Emma.

"Okay spill!" Her best friend Amy said, leaning across the table. Amy was a little girl with more energy and spunk than anyone of her small size should have. With her long blonde hair and beautiful green eyes she was the quintessential cheerleader. Why she was friends with Emma was anyone's guess.

Emma blinked, totally clueless as to what Amy was talking about.

"Spill what?" She asked.

Emma opened her backpack and pulled out the brown paper bag which held her lunch. She couldn't stand the cafeteria food, the cheese they used tasted too much like rubber for her comfort and the amount of grease on the rest of it made her sick just to think about it. She had been packing her own lunch for school since second grade and nothing she ever saw in the cafeteria made her want to change her mind.

"The hottie I saw you talking to! Who is he? How did you meet him? Do you like him? Was he flirting with you? Is he nice? I want all the details!" Amy whispered excitedly. Her bright green eyes practically glowed with her excitement to hear some juicy gossip. Amy was the eyes and ears of the school, she knew everything about everyone and there was nothing she loved more than to be the first person to hear new gossip.

"His name is Jason, and yes, he's nice." Emma whispered, trying not to blush.

Emma glanced around, hoping no one was listening to their conversation.

"Come on Emma," Amy cajoled, "You're the only one who's talked to him so far, what's he like? Tell me everything, starting with how you met him."

"Alright, fine." Emma said with a laugh. "But it's kind of embarrassing so please don't tell anyone."

"With you every story is embarrassing." Amy pointed out, taking a bite of her sandwich. "But I promise I won't tell anyone."

"Not everything is embarrassing!" Emma protested, rummaging through her lunch bag for her sandwich.

"Really?" Amy asked between bites. "What about the story of you at the water park? Or the one about the dance recital?"

"Those are two very bad examples." Emma defended herself. "And the choreographer really should have been a bit clearer about where the edge of the stage was."

"He probably figured it was one of those obvious things that didn't need to be explained, he didn't realize what it meant to have you as a student." Amy replied drily. "Now tell me your new embarrassing story!"

As Emma and Amy ate their lunches Emma recounted her mad dash to get to class on time and how she had ran into Jason at full speed only to get knocked off her feet and have him catch her before she hit the floor. When she told Amy of how he had asked her to walk him to his class Amy squealed in delight and when Emma told her that he wanted to meet for lunch Amy bounced up and down excitedly.

"He likes you! This is so great!" Amy exclaimed.

"No, he doesn't like me. He's just new here and I'm the only person he knows. Of course he would want to sit with me, he doesn't have anyone else to sit with." Emma shrugged. She wasn't going to let herself get excited over something that was really nothing.

"Oh, he's definitely interested." Amy said confidently, "I know these things."

"Just don't embarrass me if we do see him, okay?" Emma said.

"I don't think I could do a better job of embarrassing you than you have already done yourself." Amy replied with a smirk.

Emma scowled at Amy but her friend had already been distracted by something that was going on a few tables away from them.

"Oh look! Jessie and Chris got back together!" Amy exclaimed. "You know this is the third time they've broken up and gotten back together in the last three months? So much drama between the two of them, it's no wonder they keep breaking up."

Emma barely glanced at the girl sitting on her boyfriend's lap that Amy nodded towards. They looked like one of those annoyingly sappy couples whose relationships never lasted long enough to bother remembering. As Amy continued her stream of rumor mill gossip Emma scanned the room looking for Jason.

She had a few false alarms when she saw other tall dark haired boys but none of them were him. She was just about to give up hope that she would find him when she finally noticed him across the cafeteria sitting at a table by himself, looking around like he was expecting someone.

"Hey Amy, I'll be back in a few minutes. Will you watch my stuff?" Emma asked.

Amy followed the direction of Emma's gaze, her smile turning mischievous when she saw Jason. "Of course, go get Mr. Hottie and bring him back here so I can meet him!" She commanded.

Emma nodded absently as she stood up, barely hearing what Amy had said. Weaving and dodging her way through the shifting crowd of rambunctious teenagers Emma made her way as quickly as possible across the cafeteria. Jason still hadn't noticed her, he was looking off in the other direction.

Emma was just ten feet away from him when suddenly Morgan stepped in front of her, blocking Emma's way. Morgan's two best friends, or lackeys would be a better description, Chelsea and Kaylee, stepped up on either side of her forming a living wall between Emma and Jason. Sometimes Emma referred to them as the Barbie's in her head because all three of them were tall leggy blondes with million dollar smiles and great bodies. They also all had the emotional and mental depth of a Petri dish.

"Where do you think you're going?" Morgan asked nastily. "Your table is on the other side of the room, this is my side."

"Okay, first off, there are no sides." Emma said, rolling her eyes. "You and I just happen to sit on opposite sides of the cafeteria because that's as far away from each other as we can get. And secondly, I just came over to say hi to a friend so you don't need to get all territorial." Emma looked over Morgan's shoulder at Jason. Morgan looked over her shoulder just in time to see Jason waving Emma over.

"Don't even think about it." Morgan snapped.

"Excuse me?" Emma crossed her arms over her chest.

"The new guy is mine." Morgan announced. "Trust me, I'm doing you a favor." Morgan looked Emma up and down, clearly not impressed by what she saw. "He is way out of your league."

"We're just friends." Emma mumbled, hating herself for blushing.

"Well don't try to be friends with him, you're just going to humiliate yourself and make him uncomfortable. The last thing I need is my chances with him ruined because my freak show adopted sister did something stupid." Morgan said nastily.

Emma glanced over Morgan's shoulder at Jason again, who had half risen from his seat as if he was going to come over. The expression on her face must have given something away because his welcoming smile faded away into a confused expression. He looked between her and Morgan, clearly sensing something was going on between them. Morgan shifted to block Emma's view.

"Go back to your table." She said, clearly enunciating every word like she thought Emma was stupid. "Now!"

Emma glared at Morgan. For a moment she considered pushing past her to go to Jason but Morgan crossed her arms over her chest as Chelsea and Kaylee both stepped up next to her, forming a human wall. Morgan raised an eyebrow, staring down her nose at Emma. Emma expelled a frustrated breath and reluctantly turned around to walk back to her table. She glanced back after she had walked a few feet away and saw Morgan and her friends descend on Jason, all fake smiles and tossing hair. They may be shallow and vicious but the three of them were all gorgeous and Emma wouldn't blame any guy for preferring to eat lunch with them over her.

When Emma dejectedly slumped onto the bench at the table Amy didn't even wait to give her a chance to speak.

"What the heck happened?" She demanded, one small hand slapping the table hard enough to make Emma jump.

"Morgan happened." Emma replied, tiredly rubbing her forehead. She always got headaches after these sorts of encounters with Morgan.

26

"What do you mean 'Morgan happened'." Amy snapped. Amy was so incensed her pointy little nose was twitching.

"I mean Morgan told me to back off, that she had claimed him and she was doing me a favor because there is no way a girl like me would ever have a chance with a guy like him." Emma repeated Morgan's words in a monotone voice. She stared at the brown bag that held the remains of her lunch but she had no interest in eating anymore.

"And you didn't slap her across her skinny little face and tell her off?" Amy asked, her expression outraged.

"Amy you know Morgan, if I cross her she makes my life a living hell. It's just easier to stay out of her way." Emma sighed, dropping her head onto her folded arms on the table.

Emma looked across the cafeteria at the table where Jason sat surrounded by Morgan and her friends. He was looking at Emma, despite Morgan's best attempts to distract him. His stare didn't waver, finally it was Emma who looked away.

"Morgan is probably right." Emma said with a shrug. "It never would have worked out with us anyways."

CHAPTER THREE

Standing outside of Common Grounds waiting for Amy Emma stared intently at the antique store across the street, trying to ignore the shapes flitting in the corner of her vision. They were more obvious today than usual. She could almost see a little shape dancing around the coffee cup of the lady sitting at the table next to her.

Emma was focused so completely on the antique store than she didn't hear the footsteps coming up behind her or the shadow that covered hers. A hand landed on her shoulder, startling Emma. She whirled around, tripping over her feet as she did.

"Emma!" Amy said with a laugh, catching her friend. "I shouted your name five times. I swear, you are the only person I know who can tune out the world so entirely that you only see what is directly in front of you." Across the street a girl waved to Amy, distracting her while Emma refocused on the world around her. Amy waved ecstatically at the girl, miming that she should call her later.

"I wish I only saw what was in front of me." Emma muttered, trying not to look at the little shape next to the woman's coffee.

"What?" Amy asked, looking back at her.

Emma looked at her innocently. "Nothing." She said, quirking her eyebrows comically.

A startled exclamation burst from the woman, quickly followed by the sound of her chair clattering to the ground as she jumped to her feet, coffee staining the front of her blouse and pants. On the table her cup rolled back and forth on it's side, the last of the coffee leaking out onto the table.

"Ooohhh, good thing her coffee was iced." Amy whispered as she linked her arm with Emma's and turned to walk inside.

As they walked away Emma could have sworn she saw a little shape bent over laughing as the lady frantically grabbed napkins to clean up the mess.

Mark had seen Emma pull into the small gravel parking lot of the hipster coffee shop he worked at. Through the large front window he watched as she slid out of the car, her dark hair tumbling around her face. Stray beams of sunlight would high light her hair, showing glints of red mixed in with the dark brown. For a second she stood by her car, looking out at nothing, lost in her thoughts.

In that moment he could see her sadness and frustration. Mark frowned, not liking the look on her face. He was about to go out there and demand what was wrong when Amy walked up and grabbed Emma's arm. It was like a mask slide into place, hiding how she felt, as Emma turned to smile at Amy before they walked inside.

"Mark!" Emma called out, weaving her way through the after school crowd. "Hey! Can you believe how crowded it is in here?" She asked conversationally. She kept her eyes on his like she always did. Her intense, soul-bearing stare was something he had long since gotten used to.

"It's been busy. Not that you can tell from looking at the tip jar." He said drily. It was common knowledge that students were the worst tippers but this crowd took that stereotype to the extreme.

Emma made a sympathetic face. "Rough day?" She asked.

"Not anymore." He replied, giving her a wink. "Just give me a few minutes and I will have your drink ready for you."

"Thanks Mark! What would I do without you?" Emma asked, flashing him a grin.

"I have no idea." Mark said, shaking his head. He pointed to where Amy had found the last two available armchairs. "You should probably snag the one next to her before someone else tries to."

Emma flashed him another grin and darted off through the crowd, just barely beating someone else to the chair. He watched as she got settled in, tucking her feet up on the chair and chatting with Amy before he turned and started making her favorite drink. Five minutes later he was making his way through the crowd, Emma's drink in his hand.

"One frozen Mint Mocha Madness, for the lady." He said grandly, presenting her with the drink.

"Oooohhh good! I've been looking forward to this all day." She took a sip of the drink and hummed appreciatively. "You make the best drinks, Mark."

Mark grinned. "I add a little extra flavoring just for you, but don't tell anyone or they will be asking for it too." He whispered.

"It will be our little secret." Emma assured him, a happy smile on her face.

"I'm fine, by the way." Amy interjected, leaning forward to catch their eyes. "I didn't want anything to drink."

Emma and Mark stared at Amy blankly. Amy looked back and forth between them for a moment, then she leaned back in her chair and regally waved them on.

"Continue." She said airily, reaching over to pluck Emma's drink from her hand.

Emma rolled her eyes and Mark snorted before they turned back to each other.

"Just to give you a heads up, Morgan is here." Mark warned her.

Emma pulled a face. "Where is she?"

"In the back corner over there," Mark nodded to a large group of teenagers that were the main source of noise in the small building. "Who's that guy sitting next to her? I don't recognize him."

The crowd shifted enough to give Emma a glance at Morgan and the guy in question. Jason nodded at her from across the room and Emma gave a small wave in response. Then Emma noticed the evil glare Morgan was aiming at her and she quickly looked away.

"That's Jason, he's new here. Morgan has him in her sights to be her next victim. Or boyfriend. Whatever you want to call it." She slouched in her chair, scowling over at Morgan's group of friends.

Mark raised his eyebrows in surprise.

"Whoa, someone sounds a little bitter. What's going on there?" He asked, sitting on the armrest of Emma's chair.

"Nothing, just more Morgan drama." Emma replied with a shrug.

Mark and Amy shared a glance, then Amy batted her eyelids and glanced down at the drink she was still holding, swirling her finger around the lid. Mark looked down at the top of Emma's head and sighed. Brushing her hair to one side he slid his hand onto the back of her neck, massaging the muscles on either side of her spine.

"Mmm, that feels good." Emma murmured in a sleepy voice, dropping her head forward.

"Emma, is everything okay?" Mark asked in a casual voice, continuing the soothing massage.

Under his fingers he felt her muscles tense although she didn't move. Her voice, when she answered, was carefully neutral.

"Of course, everything is fine." She murmured.

"You know you can talk to me about anything, right?" He said softly.

Emma tilted her head to the side a little, just enough to glance at him out of the corner of her eye and smile at him. "It's stupid high school drama, nothing important. But I appreciate that you're willing to stoop to the level of giving me a massage to find out what's bothering me."

Mark laughed and stood up, dropping his hand from her neck. "That obvious?"

Emma made a noise of dissatisfaction when he stepped away and rolled her neck from one side to the other, stretching out the recently massaged muscles.

"A little." She said with a grin, rubbing the side of her neck with her right hand. "You only do it when you're trying to get me to tell you something."

Mark shook his head, looking down at his feet and hooking his thumbs in his pockets. Looking up at her from beneath his eyebrows he gave her a crooked grin. "I'm going to have to think of a new way to get you to talk to me."

Emma wrinkled her nose. "Why? This way works so well. I get a massage and you get to feel like you tricked me into talking." A mischievous smile pulled at her lips as she looked up at him, settling back in her chair and draping her arms along the armrests.

Mark smiled and rolled his eyes. "As much fun as it is to be your personal masseuse I have a job to get back to."

Emma gave him a pouty look. "You shouldn't tease a girl with massages like that, it's not very nice." She said.

"True," He agreed, nodding his head. "But at least I brought you coffee."

Emma leaned back in the deep leather armchair and considered this for a second, her expression thoughtful. Then she gave him a big smile and nodded. "You're forgiven." She said cheerfully.

"Thanks, princess." Mark said sardonically, kicking her foot but he was smiling as he turned to walk away.

Emma watched Mark as he walked away, not that it would be possible to lose sight of him. He was so tall that he stood head and shoulders above everyone else in the crowded room. She had asked him how tall he was once but all he had said was "Tall." He always did stuff like that, giving vague answers instead of real ones.

Emma watched him at the cash register ringing up a customer. His long sleeve kept slipping over his hand and he made a motion like he was about to push the sleeve up but he stopped himself before he did. She didn't know why he always wore such baggy clothes. He would look great in a fitted t-shirt. Or anything that was even remotely close to being the right size for him.

Shaking her head at the strangeness of her friend Emma turned back to Amy to say something when the door to the coffee shop opened. Wind swirled into the room and Emma froze, a chill running down her spine. She felt something, like a silent pulse that she felt through a sixth sense she didn't know she had. Around her everyone kept talking and laughing, no else seemed to have felt it but Emma had the eerie feeling that something big had just happened.

Just then a man rushed into the coffee shop. Curly brown hair tossed from the wind, his pale blue eyes scanned the room as if he was searching for someone. The man looked like he had just been tossed out of a tornado. His clothes were in complete disarray, rumpled and smudged with a few tears on the elbows of his jacket.

Emma felt a momentary pang of sympathy for the poor man. Deep circles were underneath his eyes like he hadn't slept in days and he looked just, haggard. His pale blue eyes fixed somewhere across the room and before she could blink he was pushing his way through the crowd. When she lost sight of him in the crowd Emma mentally shrugged and focused on Amy again, dismissing the man from her mind.

Over at the coffee counter Mark had just handed a client their debit card back when the door opened and the rush of energy flooded into the room. Immediately glancing in Emma's direction he saw Emma's reaction, then he scanned the room to see if anyone else had felt the strange pulse.

The only other person in the room showing any sign of noticing anything was the guy Emma had mentioned was with Morgan, Jason. Jason was staring at Emma, watching her. There was something about him, something suspicious. A stranger who showed up out of nowhere and was cozying up to Emma and Morgan the same day that a large energy flare occurred for the first time in seventeen years. Mark didn't think it was just coincidence.

"Mark!" An unfamiliar voice hissed at him.

Mark blinked, turning to face the voice. Leaning over the counter was a rumpled man with curly brown hair that looked to be in his mid-thirties. His eyes stared at Mark with such intensity that Mark had to fight the urge to step back.

"May I help you?" Mark asked. Looking down he tugged at the cuff of one sleeve, adjusting it around his wrist before glancing up at the man from beneath his lowered brows.

The man's eyes darted around the room as his hands flitted restlessly around his body. He wouldn't stop fidgeting. In the few seconds Mark watched him the man tugged at his collar, pulled at his shirt, checked his watch, and scratched at the back of his hand. At Mark's question the man made an effort to restrain himself, settling for tapping his fingers rapidly on the counter.

"My name is Tyler, Tyler White." He spoke quickly and quietly, nervously glancing over his shoulder.

The name struck a cord with Mark, he had heard it somewhere before. Mark narrowed his eyes at Tyler.

"Your name sounds familiar. Have we met?"

Tyler shook his head once, sharply. "The fact you've heard my name is…well, it means I've come to the right place. Is there somewhere we can speak privately?"

Mark looked back at Emma, making sure she was where he had left her. She was still sitting in the armchair, talking to Amy. She wasn't going to leave anytime soon. He nodded for Tyler to follow him then turned and walked to one of the backrooms, the only room in the building that slightly muffled the noise of the crowd. Mark stood by the door to the room and waited for Tyler to go inside, following him in.

"Are you sure we won't be overheard?" Tyler pressed. His gaze constantly darted from one place to the next as he shifted back and forth on his feet, like he was restraining himself from bolting.

Mark nodded. "I'm sure."

Tyler began to pace back and forth from one side of the small room to the other, wringing his hands. Lips pressed together he muttered to himself. "I suppose this will have to do. No other options…"

Mark's brow furrowed in confusion. He was about to speak when Tyler suddenly rushed towards him and grabbed both of his arms.

Mark tried to jerk back in surprise but the scruffy looking man was stronger than he looked.

"I found them!" Tyler whispered urgently. "I didn't even know what I was looking for, but I found them!"

34

Mark leaned back from him, grasping Tyler's upper arms in his own hands to ease him back a bit but Tyler didn't budge. His washed out blue eyes stared into Mark's without blinking.

"Found what?" Mark asked, trying to lean back himself.

"The Whitesmith Journals!"

Mark stilled, carefully studying the deranged man in front of him. "Those are just a legend." He said, shaking his head slowly from side to side. His eyes narrowed as he stared down at Tyler. "They don't exist."

Tyler shook his head urgently, crowding closer to Mark, his eyes shining with conviction. "No, they're real! The legends are finally coming true."

Mark froze. "What legends?" He demanded.

"The…"

The sound of someone opening the door cut Tyler off. The blood drained out of his face and he leapt away from the doorway, cowering in the far corner of the room.

"They found me!" He exclaimed in a strangled whisper.

The door to the room creaked open and Emma stuck her head into the room.

"Oh, sorry." Emma apologized, pushing her dark hair out of her face as she looked at Mark. "I was just..."

Emma's voice trailed off, an uncomfortable expression crossing her face when she saw who Mark was talking to. Mark looked over his shoulder at Tyler to see what the crazy man was doing. But Tyler was just staring at Emma, jaw dropped and eyes so wide they bugged out from his head slightly. Mark and Emma exchanged a confused look before Tyler's hoarse voice caught their attention.

"It's her!" He whispered in awe, staring at Emma.

Emma's grip on the door handle tightened slightly. "Mark?" She said hesitantly, looking to him for a clue as to what was going on.

"What do you mean, 'It's her'?" Mark shifted to put himself in Tyler's line of sight but Tyler just leaned to stare around him.

"*The one who will turn the tide.*" Tyler whispered. Awe shone in his eyes as he stared at Emma, who was becoming increasingly red in the face.

"Turn the tide? What tide?" Mark demanded, stepping closer to Tyler.

Tyler finally looked up at Mark. "The battle, who will rule next, the fate of our whole world, it's up to her."

"The fate of our world?" Emma echoed, confusion written all over her face.

"It's already beginning. Didn't you feel it?" Tyler asked them both.

Emma's eyes grew wide. She quickly stepped into the room and shut the door. "Was that the strange energy that I felt when you opened the door?" She asked excitedly.

Tyler nodded solemnly. "That was the Guardian." He murmured. "Important things are about to happen and you will be at the center of all of it."

Tyler's gaze sharpened on Emma. Then his head tilted to the side as he stared at her quizzically.

"Not right." He muttered, shaking his head and absently chewing on his fingernails. "Something's not right. She doesn't *see.*"

His eyes opened wide in revelation and he smiled gleefully. "That's it!" He exclaimed. Mark and Emma exchanged another concerned look as Tyler dug through his pockets, searching for something.

"Where is it?!?" He exclaimed to himself. "Must be here somewhere. I know it's here…Ahhh!" Tyler opened the palm of his hand and grinned triumphantly. "Perfect!"

Emma leaned towards him, curiosity prodding her to see what he was holding. She shifted a step closer, then another. She was just a few feet away from him now but she still couldn't see what he was holding in his hand. Just a little closer…

"Em." Mark growled, warning her back.

Emma turned to look back at him and in a flash Tyler had sidestepped behind her, slamming the object into the back of her neck. Emma felt a pop in her mind, a flash of sensation that was pain, but not really pain. She cried out, her knees buckling as Tyler crowed, "Now you will *see!*"

36

Mark bellowed in rage. Leaping forward he caught Emma with one arm, shoving Tyler back with the other. Emma sagged against his chest and stared in stunned shock, watching as her best friend seemed to change before her eyes. It was like he grew bigger, his hair was rougher and his teeth were sharper as he bared them in a snarl at Tyler.

He was so angry she could practically see the sparks shooting from his eyes as he pinned Tyler to the wall with his other hand. Tyler giggled uncontrollably, his crazed eyes rolling around in his head as he muttered to himself in a singsong voice…

"Who is blind but still can see, will find the map within the tree, stay the course, reverse the sands, fix the wrongs..."

"Shut up!" Mark yelled, grabbing the front of Tyler's shirt and shaking him like a rag.

Abruptly Tyler stopped giggling. "Keep her safe!" He spoke to Mark. "Alteria depends on her!"

Tyler yanked out of Mark's grip and bolted from the room.

Mark growled in annoyance, staring at the door Tyler had disappeared through. Tension radiated through his body as he fought the urge to chase after him. Slowly sinking to the ground Mark pulled Emma onto his lap, wrapping her in a hug. She sat there, eyes wide as she listened to his heart pounding in his chest. Finally Mark grunted, blowing out a breath of air as the tension eased out of his body. He looked down at Emma and tugged a strand of her hair to get her to look up at him.

"You okay?" He asked.

Emma gave him a weak smile. "Yeah." She murmured. "I think so anyways."

Emma struggled to stand up and Mark assisted her, pushing himself to his feet as well.

"What was that?" Emma asked Mark, rubbing the back of her neck.

Mark shrugged. "I have no idea, but if you ever see him again I want you to stay away from him."

"I kind of thought he was interesting." Emma commented.

Mark gaped at her. "He attacked you! *And* he was just saying gibberish." Mark replied harshly.

Emma smiled ruefully, rubbing the back of her neck. "Yes, but it was *interesting* gibberish."

Mark grunted. "Do you know what he pressed against your neck?" He asked, looking down at her.

Emma held her hand out between them and slowly opened her fingers to reveal a small metal disk lying on her palm. Strange symbols were etched into the dull metal but besides that there was nothing remarkable about it.

Emma shrugged. "I'm not exactly sure what it is."

Mark scowled. "You should throw it away."

"Throw it away? Why would I do that?" Surprise laced Emma's voice. She quickly closed her fingers around the metal disk and shoved it in her pocket.

"Because he's crazy. You don't know what that thing is." Mark argued.

"Whatever he was going to do with it has been done. What if he did do something and this thing is the key to reversing it?" Emma argued back.

Mark threw his hands up in the air. "Fine. Keep it." He said, scowling at her.

Emma crossed her arms and looked down her nose at Mark. "I will."

Mark was about to snap a reply when the door to the backroom opened. "Emma?" Amy's voice drifted over to them. "What are you two doing back here? And who was that guy?" Amy stuck her head in the room, her blue eyes looking at them curiously.

"No one." Mark snapped.

Amy's eyebrows raised in surprise and she gave a low whistle at Mark's angry response. Mark watched Emma chew on her lower lip distractedly, unconsciously pushing back the bangs that stubbornly insisted on falling into her eyes every few seconds. She was so innocent, unable to comprehend the idea of hurting anyone or that anyone would want to hurt her. Mark wanted her to remain that way as long as possible.

Emma looked up and saw him staring at her. She made a face at him and grinned, her smile so infectious he found it difficult not to smile back. When she turned to walk back into the main room with Amy, Mark's resolve grew, he would keep her safe no matter what the cost. But in order to do that he needed more information.

Back in the main room Emma and Amy began to walk back to their chairs but Amy saw a friend and ran over to talk to them. Emma shrugged and sat down by herself. Leaning back in the armchair she was sitting she placed her mocha on the side table next to her and ran her index finger up and down the seam of the cup as she thought about the strange conversation she had walked in on. She didn't even notice that Jason had walked up and was standing right next to her.

"You look deep in thought."

Emma jerked in surprise, nearly knocking over her recently recovered drink. She pressed a hand to her chest, feeling her heart beating a mile a minute. She slowly turned, tilting her head to glance up at Jason.

"Hey Jason, I didn't hear you walk up." She said casually, leaning forward to quickly grab her drink to steady it. She eyed him curiously, wondering what he was doing over here instead of at the back of the shop with Morgan.

Jason chuckled. "I can see that. Do you always jump so high when someone comes up behind you?"

"Only when I'm not expecting them." Emma said, scanning the coffee shop for any sign of disapproving countenance. She looked back at Jason and he raised an eyebrow at her. "So yeah, almost every time." She conceded. Leaning back she crossed her arms over her chest and gave him a dark look. "You should really stop sneaking up on me like that."

"That easily scared, huh?" Jason teased.

"Not scared, startled. There's a difference. I don't get scared." Emma corrected him.

A shadow appeared in the corner of her eye and Emma flinched away. The boy who was walking past her chair gave her a strange look but continued to walk past.

"Of course." Jason said dryly, looking back and forth between Emma and the other boy. "So what happened at lunch?"

Jason asked, snagging an unoccupied stool from a nearby table and moving it so he could sit in front of her.

Emma gave him a confused look. "What do you mean?"

"We were supposed to have lunch together. Remember?" Jason prodded.

Emma looked down at her lap at her hands that were folded together. "Oh yeah, I must have forgotten. Sorry about that." Emma lied, wincing at how lame that sounded even in her own ears.

Jason looked down at her skeptically. "Really? Because I thought I saw you staring at me."

Emma looked up, her eyebrows raised in surprise. "Was I?" She asked, tilting her head to the side. "That's weird, I don't remember seeing you."

Jason's gaze narrowed on her face, then he shrugged and leaned back on the stool. "Okay, well if you do ever want to talk or come over and eat lunch with us...you can."

Emma blinked, surprised at his offer but his attention wasn't on her anymore. Jason was staring somewhere behind her, he hardly looked like he was even paying attention to their conversation. Emma smiled a little at the idea of how Morgan would react if Emma just sat down at their table for lunch one day.

"I don't think my sister would like that." She replied, taking a sip of her mocha.

"Your sister?" Jason sounded so confused Emma almost laughed.

"Morgan." Emma told him. His eyes widened in shock as he stared at her, then looked over to where Morgan sat, then back at her.

"Really?" He asked. When Emma nodded he was quiet for a moment, then he shrugged and threw Emma a charming smile.

"Isn't annoying each other what siblings do?" Jason asked teasingly.

"Yeah, that's more of a one direction thing with us." Emma said distractedly. She was scanning the coffee shop wondering where Amy had run off to. When Jason shot her a questioning look Emma explained grudgingly. "I learned a while ago it's not worth the hassle to annoy her."

"You're right, you're probably out of your league taking on Morgan."

That startled a laugh out of Emma. "Scare me and then insult me, I see Morgan has been rubbing off on you." Emma leaned back in the armchair as Jason slowly grinned.

"I thought you said that you don't get scared." Jason reminded her.

"I don't, but I wasn't scared for me. You almost made me spill my coffee, I was scared for *you*." Emma replied.

Jason laughed. He propped a foot up on the stool and leaned an arm on it, looking down at Emma with his deep blue eyes. "Okay, I'm sorry. I didn't mean to make you almost spill your drink."

"Thank you." Emma said, giving him a gracious nod.

There was a slight pause as they sat there in silence. Emma looked at Jason and could immediately see what it was that appealed to Morgan. He was just wearing a plain dark jacket, white shirt, and dark blue jeans but he seemed so completely sure of himself that anyone could tell he did what he wanted, when he wanted. Which of course, made him an irresistible challenge to Morgan. Emma on the other hand was a little more wary of him.

Jason stretched a leg out to nudge her foot with his. Emma raised her eyebrows at the motion, looking at him inquisitively.

"Why are you sitting over here by yourself?" Jason asked, his head slightly tilted to the side. He watched her carefully, like she was a puzzle he was trying to figure out. Emma shifted uncomfortably, crossing her legs as she took a drink of her mocha.

"I'm not by myself." She said lightly. "My friend would just rather talk to other people." She nodded her head over at Amy who was making the rounds through the crowd, talking to one person and whispering with the next. Jason looked over at her and raised his eyebrows, nodding thoughtfully. "Mark also comes over and talks to me when he has time." She added. Emma looked over at the counter, trying to see Mark but he was hidden behind a line of customers.

"Is Mark the guy that I saw talking to you earlier?" Jason asked casually. He propped both feet up on the stool and leaned forward towards Emma.

"Yeah…you noticed him?" Emma asked, surprised. She took another sip of her mocha, watching him over the top of the cup. Something shifted in his expression, his eyes became slightly more distant, a little more careful. He took a moment to reply.

"I noticed when you walked in and he just happened to be talking to you at the time." Jason explained, shifting back slightly. Emma narrowed her eyes at his response but she nodded, accepting the answer.

"Okay." She murmured, watching the tension ease from him when she didn't press him further. Emma scanned the room, keeping track of Amy and Mark but also just seeing who was there. Across the room Morgan and her friends were shooting death glares at Emma, clearly unhappy Jason was talking to her. Emma smiled and waved at them, receiving a haughty head toss from Morgan in return. "I don't think Morgan likes you being over here." She commented, her lips twisting in a wry smile.

Jason looked over at Morgan and saw the dirty looks she was aiming at Emma. "I just don't think she likes me talking to you period." Jason's brow furrowed in confusion as he looked back and forth between Morgan and Emma. "So what is the deal with you two? Why does she hate you so much?"

"She doesn't hate me." Emma said lightly. "She just can't stand me."

"That's much better," Jason said drily, "I have no idea how I mistook that for hatred."

"It's a common mistake." Emma reassured him. She paused for a moment, staring pensively at her adopted sister who was whispering to one of the other blondes. Karly, or Kimber, whatever her name was. "As for why, there isn't really a reason. She just always has, ever since we were kids."

"When did your parents adopt you?" Jason asked abruptly, shifting forward again.

Emma's gaze shot back to him, startled by the question. He was watching her intently, open curiosity in his face.

"You don't mind asking the personal questions, do you?" Emma said teasingly but she on the inside she felt frozen, her entire body opposed to the idea of talking to him about this.

42

"I didn't know it was a personal question." Jason replied. His voice had softened, like he was trying not to startle her. Emma appreciated the attempt but it was a little late for that.

"I guess it probably wouldn't be if the circumstances weren't what they are." Emma murmured. She looked over at Morgan again but Morgan had rejoined the conversation with her friends, restraining herself to only the occasional death glare in Emma's direction.

"So what were the circumstances?" Jason prodded.

Emma's expression grew distant as she remembered the last night she had seen her parents. By now she only remembered bits and pieces of that night, the fear in her mother's green eyes, and her father's strong arms as he carried her inside the Wellworth's house. What she remembered most was the overwhelming feeling that something was not right. When her father had tried to hand her to Steve, Emma had burst into tears and refused to let go of him.

Maybe a part of her knew that would be the last time she would see her parents. The last thing she remembered were her parents walking away, her father's arm around her mother as she looked back at Emma with tears in her eyes. It was a whole year before the police found her parents car at the bottom of a ravine and declared them dead.

"Emma?"

Emma was jerked back to reality by Jason's face in front of hers. He was no longer on the stool but kneeling in front of her, a worried look on his face. She attempted a reassuring smile but from the way he narrowed his eyes at her she didn't think he bought it. Jason placed a hand on her knee and it was as if a jolt went through her entire system.

Not in the romantic, butterflies-in-the-stomach kind of way. It was more like touching a live electric fence around a cattle pasture. Jason's eyes widened in shock and he snatched his hand away while Emma sat there, stunned. For a moment they stared at each other, frozen in shock. Emma's pulse pounded in her ears. Snapping her jaw closed she took a deep breath, trying to control her frantically beating heart.

"It's actually a boring story." She rushed to tell him before he could say anything. Emma glanced at her watch and gave Jason an apologetic look. "I'm really sorry but I need to go, I have a job interview at five." She quickly stood up and grabbed her purse. "Oh, you should probably talk to Morgan. She has been trying to get your attention for a while now."

Jason stood with her, obviously confused by the sudden end to their conversation and what had happened. He turned to look at Morgan who immediately waved him over with an urgent expression. "Will you at least call me…" Jason said as he turned back to face Emma but she was already walking out the door.

Jason looked confused at her abrupt exit. "I'll talk to you tomorrow then." He muttered to himself.

Jason stood there for a moment, staring at the door Emma had just disappeared through. Then Morgan caught his eye again and waved him over, more insistently this time. Jason hesitated, looking back at the door Emma had disappeared through. With a sigh he turned and walked back to Morgan.

CHAPTER FOUR

The bookstore that Mrs. White owned, Bookends, was a cute little bookstore next to the coffee shop where Mark worked. The shelves were filled with old classic books, leather bound editions and books with handcrafted illustrations.

Deep leather armchairs were scattered throughout the store with reading lamps set on tables next to them and all the furniture was dark wood. An air of stillness filled the store, as if the books would whisper their secrets to her if she would just sit and be patient enough to listen.

Emma loved the bookstore from the moment she walked into it. As she stood by the counter waiting for Mrs. White, who she could hear moving around in the backroom Emma looked around enjoying the atmosphere of the store. After a few minutes Mrs. White shuffled into the room carrying a precariously stacked pile of books that was so high Emma could only see a tuft of white curly hair behind them.

Emma coughed politely.

"Oh! Hello, dear!" Mrs. White exclaimed, peering around the stack of books. "Just give me one second and I will help you."

"Do you need any help?" Emma asked, looking on in concern as the stack of books wobbled and almost fell.

"No no dear, I've got it. I just need to put them down right…here!" Mrs. White said in a satisfied voice as she successfully slid the stack of books onto the counter. "Now, how may I help you?" She said briskly, brushing off her hands and peering at Emma with shrewd brown eyes.

"My name is Emma Rose," Emma introduced herself, holding out her hand. "My mother Kathryn told me you were looking for someone to work in the store part time."

"Yes, your mother called and told me you would be coming by today. It's nice to meet you dear!" Mrs. White said, shaking her hand. "My name is Mrs. White."

As they shook hands Emma couldn't help but smile at the image that Mrs. White portrayed. She was a plump little lady with short, wildly curly hair that was pure white and warm brown eyes that shone with kindness. Her eyes held a certain shrewd intelligence though. She was the perfect image of what a grandmother should look like, the sort of woman whose picture would be put on the front of a bakery or pastry store. Emma liked her immediately.

"I'm afraid it wouldn't be very exciting work," Mrs. White said apologetically. "As you can see there aren't usually many customers in the store at any given time and I can only pay you minimum wage."

Emma shrugged and gave her a smile. "Minimum wage is fine, and as long as I'm allowed to look through the books I don't think I would ever get bored working here."

Mrs. White beamed. "I just love books, I don't see how anyone could find reading boring but apparently not everyone agrees with me. Oh well, if you are a fellow book lover then I would love to have you work here. When can you start?"

"I can start tomorrow if you need me." Emma replied, slightly surprised at how quickly Mrs. White had offered her the job.

"Perfect!" Mrs. White exclaimed, clapping her hands together sharply. "We will discuss what hours you will work and everything tomorrow, for today let me show you around."

Emma grinned cheerfully, caught up by Mrs. White's infectious enthusiasm. She followed as Mrs. White led her around the store, pointing out where everything was.

After they made the circuit of the main room Mrs. White took Emma behind the counter and showed her the backrooms where her office was and the room where she stored the extra books. At the end of the hallway there was a back entrance door that led to the access road behind the bookstore.

"The only time I ever use that door is to throw the trash bags in the dumpster back there, so that door remains locked for the most part." Mrs. White explained. "Maybe I've read too many classic horror stories but that back access road just seems like the perfect setting for a murder mystery and that is one kind of story I would rather not have a leading role in."

When they walked back out into the main room Emma noticed a small room separated from the main room by an open doorway with thick red drapes artistically framing the opening. She could just get the barest glimpse of a narrow staircase in the back of the room leading down somewhere she couldn't see.

"What's in that room?" Emma asked.

"What room?" Mrs. White asked, looking confused.

"The room right there through the red drapes." Emma said, pointing to it. "You didn't show me that area."

"Oh right, that room." Mrs. White said, as if finally figuring out what Emma was talking about. "That's nothing special. I just keep a bunch of miscellaneous books in there."

"What about the staircase?" Emma pressed.

"That goes nowhere, just an old room with a locked door that no one has the key to. This store has been in my family for generations and that key has been lost for at least the last three. I don't even know what's in that room."

Mrs. White's smile wavered a bit and she looked off to the side, away from Emma. Emma eyed her suspiciously, but she kept her expression open and her tone carefully even when she said, "If you ever get curious you could always call a locksmith to open it."

"No dear," Mrs. White said with a smile, meeting Emma's eyes for a moment and looking away again, "I like the mystery of it. A locked door in the basement of a bookstore that has been owned by the same family for centuries, it sounds so eerie don't you think?"

Emma laughed and shook her head. "You love old mystery and horror stories, don't you?"

"I do, they wrote them so much better back when there was no explanations for what went bump in the night beyond pure imagination." Mrs. White said with a sigh, walking Emma back to the front of the store.

"There is still some mystery in the world," Emma said helpfully. "Science hasn't explained everything."

"Indeed it has not." Mrs. White agreed. "And for that I am very grateful."

Mrs. White and Emma reached the front desk and the end of Emma's tour.

"Well!" Mrs. White said, clapping her hands together. "Now you've had a tour of the store, if you come back at the same time tomorrow we can get started with all the boring work details."

"That sounds great." Emma agreed. "I will see you at five o'clock tomorrow."

Emma waved as she walked out the door and headed to her car. When Emma was out of sight Mrs. White walked into the small back room and stood next to the staircase that Emma had noticed. Staring down at it Mrs. White murmured. "How did she see you?"

Emma sat in her car for a moment and thought about what waited for her at home. Morgan would probably be sulking in the television room already. Steve had decided Morgan needed to come home for family dinners during the week. Part of his attempt to save what little bit of humanity was still in her, assuming there had been any there to begin with.

If Emma went home now she would have to listen to Morgan talk nonstop about Jason. Just the thought of it made her feel physically sick. Emma already knew it had been a mistake to let Morgan chase her away at lunch. She wasn't going to let Morgan rub her face in her mistake, even if that meant driving around town aimlessly to avoid going home.

As Emma sat lost in these thoughts she was abruptly pulled back to reality by her ringing phone. Emma reached into her purse with one hand and snagged her phone, flipping it over to see who it was. A picture of Amy filled the screen.

"Hey Amy." Emma answered the phone. She leaned back in her seat and rolled down a window to let some fresh air into the car. "What's up?"

"Are you done with your after school work thing?" Amy asked, her tone making it apparent the 'work thing' was merely an inconvenience, like detention but less interesting. Emma rolled her eyes. Amy had a fantastic mind for details when it came to gossip but anything as mundane and boring as a job interview was just glossed over.

"Yeah, I just walked out." Emma answered as she turned on the car and started messing with the radio. Something in front of her car caught her eye and Emma looked up to see a tiny…fairy? Emma squeezed her eyes shut, hoping that she was just seeing things but when she opened them again, there it was. It was flitting around the windshield wipers of her car, poking at a leaf that had gotten stuck.

Emma leaned closer to the windshield to get a better look at the creature. It looked like a tiny boy. It wore tiny little pants that were ripped and ragged at the bottom and no shirt. Something was strapped against its back, held in place by a broad leather strap that crossed his chest and buckled just beneath his collarbone. Dark wings sprouted from his back. Not the delicate gossamer wings that fairies in children's stories had that looked whimsical and beautiful. These wings had black spines swirling in intricate designs through a translucent black membrane. At the top and bottom of the wings the spines curved up into sharp dagger like points. Along the sides of the wings the dark spines thickened into a bonelike form. She watched the fairy use the spike at the bottom of its wing to stab the leaf and drag it out from under the windshield wiper.

"Perfect! You should come over right now. I already asked my mom and she said you can stay for dinner." Amy said cheerfully.

Emma watched the fairy in shock, afraid to move in case she somehow caught it's attention. "Uh huh." She said to Amy distractedly.

The fairy grabbed the leaf off of its wing and opened it up to look at the inside of it. It tilted the leaf one way, then another, studying it carefully. Almost as if it was…reading it? Emma thought that's what it was doing anyways. Suddenly the fairy cocked its head to one side as if it had heard something.

The fairy paused, listening to the noise Emma couldn't hear. Then it threw the leaf aside and leapt into the air, its wings snapping open to catch the slight afternoon breeze. The wind caught the fairy and in seconds it was out of sight.

"Hello? Emma? Stop playing with the radio when we're talking, you aren't that good at multi-tasking." Amy admonished.

"What?" Emma said, refocusing on the conversation. "Oh, right. Sorry. What was the question?"

"Dinner. My house. Tonight. You're coming." Amy said. "And I can still hear the radio."

Emma made a face but she turned the volume down. She paused for a moment, tapping her fingers on the steering wheel as she considered her options. Go home to Morgan taunting her all night or go over to Amy's and have a delicious dinner.

"I'm on my way over." Emma said, turning the key and starting the ignition. She looked around the parking lot carefully for signs of any other fairies or strange creatures but she didn't see anything out of the ordinary.

"Great! We have a lot to talk about." Amy exclaimed.

Emma paused, frowning. It always worried her when Amy said things like that. Half the time it meant Amy wanted to tell Emma every piece of gossip she had heard that day but the other half of the time Amy wanted to talk about Emma's life. Emma didn't know if she felt up to that, especially since things had started getting even weirder lately. Their conversation a few weeks ago when she had confessed to Amy that she felt like she was being watched was one thing, it was a completely different thing to tell her she was seeing fairies reading the leaves caught under her windshield wipers.

Hanging out with Amy was better than facing Morgan, so she told Amy she would see her in a few minutes and hung up. With any luck something had happened for Amy to obsess over that would distract her from focusing on Emma's life.

Later that night when Emma got home she quietly snuck past the television room where Morgan sat watching one of her ridiculous reality TV shows, and the kitchen where Kathryn was busy cleaning up after dinner. Emma breathed a sigh of relief when she got to the stairs and no one tried to stop her, she wasn't in the mood to talk to anyone.

After dinner Amy had regaled Emma with the tale of how Brad had asked her to formal. Emma had been excited for her friend but she just couldn't get into dress shopping that night. Ever since that run in with Tyler at the coffee shop she had been feeling strange, and it was just getting worse.

Emma had just slipped into her room when her phone went off in her purse. Digging it out of her purse she checked to see who the message was from. It was from Mark. "How did the rest of your day turn out?"

She quickly typed, "Fine." And dropped her phone on her desk. Walking over to her bed she let herself fall backwards onto it with a groan. Fine. That's what her life always was. That's all she could ever let people see. Sweet Emma Rose was always fine, everything was okay, nothing was ever wrong. Emma was getting tired of just being "fine".

She heard her phone go off again as Mark replied but she didn't look at it. The truth was that she wasn't fine. Something was wrong with her. Or rather, she amended ruefully, something besides the usual was wrong with her. She gazed at the ceiling of her room, a plain white expanse with only the light fixture breaking the monotony.

Her head felt strange, like it was too full and her hands itched to do something, but she didn't know what. Emma didn't like it when things changed and she didn't know why. She wasn't a control freak, but when it came to her own mind and body unexpected changes worried her.

Her mind. Emma must be losing it. That was the only explanation for that creature she had seen earlier. That fairy hadn't been some shadow, and it certainly didn't look like a figment of her imagination. Emma had clearly seen it right in front of her. But no one else in the area had noticed it.

Unless someone had called it. From the way it had turned its head like it had heard something, Emma was fairly certain that's why it had left the way it had. Emma thought about the way the fairy had been analyzing the leaf like it was some sort of message until she realized that she was thinking about it like it had been a real thing. Emma shook her head at herself.

The line between what was real and what was imaginary was becoming so blurred she was afraid it wouldn't be long before she couldn't tell the two apart. Emma stared at the ceiling, thinking about what would happen to her when they finally officially declared her insane.

She didn't know how long she lay there staring at the ceiling thinking of everything and nothing, but eventually she made herself get up and go over to her desk. No matter how she was feeling right now; life would continue on tomorrow and that meant she had homework to do.

The next morning when Emma woke up she felt strange. There was a buzzing in her head that wasn't a noise but a sensation, like a vibration within her brain. Emma groaned and squinted at her clock. 6:00 shone back in bright blue numbers. Emma frowned, she wasn't supposed to wake up for another thirty minutes. Emma tried to roll over and go back to sleep but it was no use, the buzzing in her head wouldn't let her.

Giving up on sleep Emma stumbled to the bathroom and splashed cold water in her face hoping that would clear up her head. Emma stared at her reflection in the mirror. She looked the same but different somehow, like something had changed but she didn't know what. The cold water helped a little bit, the buzzing receded until it was only faintly present. Since she was already up Emma decided she might as well start getting ready. Emma quickly brushed her hair and even did her make-up, finishing just before Kathryn called her down to breakfast.

At breakfast she ignored the slight taunts Morgan threw her way. Emma didn't care about anything Morgan said, she was too distracted by the buzzing in her head and the fact that no matter how much she ate she was still hungry. Two large omelets, three slices of buttered toast, an apple, and two glasses of orange juice later Emma finally got up and took her plate to the sink. She turned around to find Kathryn, Steve, and Morgan staring at her.

"What?" She asked, self-consciously folding her arms across her stomach, which still wasn't full.

"Nothing," Steve replied carefully, "We've just never seen you eat so much before."

"You are normally such a delicate eater." Kathryn added. "I didn't think you were capable of eating that much."

"You're a freak." Was all Morgan said, brushing past Emma to put her dishes in the sink.

"I was just really hungry today." Emma replied defensively. When Kathryn and Steve continued to stare at her, and even Morgan was eyeing her strangely, Emma blurted, "I have to go to school now." And she quickly made her exit.

Two days later after a frustrating day at school Emma peeled out of the school parking lot. Nothing good had happened that day. A near constant headache and the strange buzzing in her head had kept her distracted the whole day. Apparently the teachers could sense her distraction because each one of them chose her as their favorite target for the day.

For each of the questions they asked she stared at them, clueless as to what they were talking about. Three of her teachers gave her additional homework to do to help her learn the material better since she was obviously struggling and the other three just settled for giving her disapproving glares.

Then, on top of the headaches and the buzzing in her head, Emma also spent the entire day feeling hungrier than she ever had in her entire life. The lunch she normally packed for herself, a sandwich with chips, an apple, and a cookie hardly even made a dent in her appetite. She had to go buy lunch in the cafeteria. As if the stares she got from other students when they saw how full her tray was wasn't bad enough, Emma tripped right as she was walking past the table where Morgan and Jason were eating lunch.

Food went everywhere, a large portion of it staining the front of her shirt. Morgan, of course, pointed and laughed at her, making sure that everyone saw. Luckily the cafeteria ladies also saw the whole embarrassing thing and took pity on her, letting her grab another serving of the food that had been ruined when she tripped.

After eating that food as quickly as she could, somehow managing to swallow past the lump of humiliation in her throat, Emma ran out to her car to grab an extra shirt that she had in there.

When she put it on she remembered that the reason it was left in her car was the huge hole in the side but she was already late to class and it was better than the pizza stains that were all over the front of the other shirt.

The extra time she spent running to her car and back meant she ran in to her next class after the bell. The teacher counted her tardy and told her that if she was late to class one more time she would get Saturday detention. If she got Saturday detention one more time Steve was going to ground her.

Not that it really made much of a difference, Emma didn't go out much anyways but she just didn't like knowing she wasn't allowed to do anything. It was okay that she didn't have a life if it was her choice, as soon as she was told she couldn't *that* was when she wanted to go out.

Emma got to the coffee shop in record time that day, which might have been because she was driving at least 20 over the speed limit the entire way there. Emma jumped out of the car, nearly getting tangled in her seatbelt in her haste. Her entire body felt wired, like she had just chugged a giant energy drink on an empty stomach. Emma's stomach growled and she rubbed her stomach with a grimace.

Emma quickly walked inside, nearly running into someone when she darted through the door.

"Watch it!" The man snapped, glaring at her indignantly.

"Sorry, I'm so sorry." Emma said over her shoulder as she hurried over to the counter and stood at the end of the line. Only two people were in front of her but Emma could hardly keep herself still. Her impatience at standing still was quickly getting the best of her self-control and she began to get very annoyed at the girl in front of her who couldn't decide on what stupid drink to order. A stab of pain hit her head, the headaches were hitting her any time she got overly excited today. Which happened to be about every five minutes or so.

Mark gave her a strange look as she stood still for a moment, holding her head between her hands against the pain. When it passed she returned to bouncing up and down on the balls of her feet. Emma tried to restrain herself but only succeeded into confining the jitters into one foot, which tapped a million times a minute. After what seemed like forever, though was probably only three minutes, the girl finally made her order and moved out of Emma's way. Emma jumped forward to stand in front of Mark.

"Hey Mark!" She said, wincing at how overly excited she sounded.

"Heyyy." Mark said much more slowly. "Are you okay? You seem really…"

"Hyper? Energetic? Peppy?" Emma supplied.

"I was going to say on edge." Mark replied. "But those work too."

"I'm fine. Great. Fantastic." Emma said, each word seeming to leap off her tongue. Realizing she was just making herself look even more off balance Emma quickly shut her mouth, preventing further words from jumping out.

"Right." Mark said dubiously. "Maybe you should skip on the coffee today…"

"What? No! I'm fine. Really." Using all of her willpower Emma made herself stand still and be calm. "See, no jitters."

"Alright fine, do you want your usual then?" Mark asked, clearly unhappy about it but not willing to argue with her.

"Yes, the usual." Emma said. Then her eyes latched hungrily onto the pastries displayed behind the glass counter. "And I want one of those raspberry Danishes. And that blueberry muffin. And a slice of that coffee cake." She said, pointing at the different pastries that she wanted.

Mark frowned at her. "Did you eat lunch today?" He asked.

"Yeah, I had a great lunch. Why?" Emma asked.

"I've just never known you to eat so much." Mark said, his brow furrowed as he stared at her.

Emma shrugged, beginning to bounce up and down again. "I'm just hungry today."

"Alright, your total is $14.52." Mark said. He turned to grab the pastries as Emma dug through her purse for her wallet, pulling out fifteen dollars to hand to Mark. A minor stab of pain hit her head, Emma squinted her eyes a bit but only hesitated in her actions for a moment. Compared to the others this minor pain was hardly worth noticing. Mark noticed her wince of pain as he handed her the pastries.

"Are your headaches coming back?" He asked, concern in his eyes.

Emma nodded sheepishly. She didn't like complaining about her headaches but Mark could always tell when they were getting too bad.

"Okay, go find some place to sit and I'll bring you your drink." Mark said.

"Thanks Mark." Emma said with a grateful smile.

Holding the bag of pastries in one hand she put her wallet back in her purse and turned to scan the room for any available seats. No seats were open though, so Emma leaned against the wall and awkwardly shuffled the bag of pastries and her wallet around in her hands until she could slide the wallet back into her purse. Feeling a little self-conscious about standing there with a bag of pastries by herself Emma scanned the room again, willing someone to leave so she could take their seat.

As she waited her stomach growled, reminding Emma of how hungry she was. Unable to resist, she peeked into the pastry bag and saw the coffee cake lying on top. Reaching inside Emma tore off a piece of coffee cake and started eating as she continued to scan the room for someplace to sit.

"Here's your drink." Mark said, appearing right next to her.

Emma jumped, coughing as she inhaled bits of coffee cake in her surprise.

"Thanks." She managed to say in between coughs. She reached for the drink and took a few quick swallows, succeeding in clearing out her throat and replacing it with a brain freeze instead.

Mark laughed when Emma scrunched up her face and whimpered. "Brain freeze."

"Maybe you shouldn't drink it so fast then." He said unhelpfully.

Emma stuck out her tongue at him but that only made Mark laugh more.

"So how bad are your headaches and how often have you been getting them?" Mark asked.

"Pretty bad." Emma admitted. "I'm getting a sharp pain in my head every few minutes now."

"Okay, turn around." Mark said, grabbing the bag of pastries and her drink and setting them down on a nearby table.

56

Emma eyed the food longingly but she obediently turned around. Mark placed one hand on the back of her neck and his other hand at the top of her forehead, pausing as Emma took a deep breath in to match his breathing to hers.

Emma felt the heat of Mark's hand warm the back of her neck and her forehead. From those two points the heat spread throughout her head, relaxing the tightness she felt within her brain. Like a warm wave it washed away the tension and the pain, allowing her to think clearly again. Mark lifted his hands and Emma blinked. She looked at Mark and gave him a huge grin.

"Feeling any better?" He asked.

"Yes, *much* better." Emma said, giving him a smile. "How do you do that?" She asked him curiously, picking up her food and drink from the table.

"It's a trick I learned from my dad." Mark replied. "I think it has to do with energy balance or something."

"Whatever it is it works. Thank you!" Emma said. She gave Mark a big hug, startling a laugh out of him.

"Wow, the headaches must have been really bad this time for you to give me a hug." Mark said teasingly.

Emma made a face at him. "You have no idea." She said.

"Okay, well I need to get back to work. Try not to hit your head or anything for the next 24 hours." Mark said, turning to walk back to the counter.

"No promises." Emma called after him.

Looking down at her hands Emma sighed. Now that she had to hold her drink she didn't have a free hand to eat with. Giving up her search for an open seat as a lost cause and uncomfortable with standing awkwardly next to the wall Emma decided to walk over to the bookstore early. At least there she knew she would be able to find an open chair and a table to eat at.

When Emma walked into the bookstore the bell above the door chimed softly as the door swung open and closed. Mrs. White wasn't in the main room. Thinking that maybe she was in one of the back rooms or her office Emma called out. "Mrs. White?" but she didn't hear a response. Mrs. White probably hadn't heard her or had stepped out for a moment. Walking over to one of the chairs with a coffee table in front of it Emma sat down and settled in, placing her coffee and pastries on the table in front of her.

Within moments the coffee cake was gone and so was the raspberry Danish. Emma was quickly working her way through the blueberry muffin when she heard a sound coming from the back of the room. Emma frowned. The only thing that was back there was the staircase and Mrs. White had told her didn't lead anywhere.

Emma quietly stood up and tiptoed to the edge of the bookcase that blocked her view of the room with the staircase and peeked around it, trying to see what the sound was. At first all that Emma saw was the brown railing that surrounded the entrance to the staircase. Then Mrs. White's head appeared as she walked up the staircase, followed by a man with curly brown hair that looked vaguely familiar.

"You shouldn't have brought it here, it's too dangerous." Mrs. White was saying.

"Just for tonight." The man said. "I'll move it tomorrow."

"You should not have come back here, you will lead them straight to us."

"I didn't have a choice. They were following me. I wasn't going to be able to outrun them for much longer."

"You never should have gotten involved Tyler." Mrs. White admonished as she stepped through the gate separating the staircase from the rest of the room. "That is not what our family does."

The man stepped into the small room and Emma got a clear look at his face. It was the crazy man from the coffee shop. But he did not look crazy anymore. His eyes were clear and he was no longer twitching nervously. Emma stifled a gasp. What was he doing here? "I couldn't just sit by and do nothing. Once she told me what was going to happen…"

Mrs. White stopped walking. "She?" She asked, turning to face him. Emma's eyes widened at the look on Mrs. White's face. The cheerful quirky woman she knew was nowhere to be seen. Mrs. White stood straight, her head held high as she stared Tyler down.

It was as if regality were draped over her shoulders like a robe. Her expression cold and distant as she looked at Tyler but Emma could see centuries of wisdom in her eyes. She raised an

58

eyebrow imperiously, demanding an answer to a question it was obvious she already knew the answer to.

Tyler looked away guiltily, his lips setting in a stubborn line.

"Lady Alexandra." Mrs. White's cold tone made it clear it wasn't a question. "Tyler, that woman is dangerous! How could you even let her get near you? The secrets we keep should never be known by anyone outside of the Circle and you spoke to the most powerful Secret Seeker in the history of our kind! What were you thinking?"

"She wasn't listening to my secrets." Tyler snapped. "She was telling me hers. If she is right..."

"I don't want to hear what that woman told you." Mrs. White cut him off harshly. "You went against everything we in the Circle stand for. I will let you keep it here for the night but tomorrow I want both of you to be gone. You are no longer a member of the Circle, my protection cannot extend to you any longer."

Tyler stared at Mrs. White for a moment, his nostrils flaring in annoyance. Without a word he turned and stormed out the back door. Mrs. White watched until the door swung shut behind him. The stiffness left her spine and Mrs. White's shoulders drooped as she dropped her head forward. She shuffled into her office and quietly shut the door.

Curiosity peaked, Emma waited until she heard the door to Mrs. White's office close firmly before she snuck into the small back room with the staircase. Something very important was obviously being kept down there and Emma wanted to know what it was.

The staircase faced the back of the room and was sunk into the floor, with just a plain wooden railing around it. Emma circled around until she stood at the top of the steps and looked down. What are they keeping down there?

The staircase was narrow and made of very old wood. It didn't seem to match the rest of the store. For some reason it seemed older, as if it had been there for much longer. Emma couldn't see what was at the bottom of the staircase though. Halfway down the staircase was lost in shadows so thick she would need a flashlight to see.

Emma lifted her hand to open the small wooden gate set at the top of the staircase. Her hand rested on the smooth, cool wood as Emma took a deep breath in, smelling the dusty smell of the old books surrounding her and the stale air of the staircase. Finally getting up her courage Emma began pushing open the gate.

"Emma? What are you doing here so early?"

Mrs. White's voice cut through the still air and Emma's hand jerked back from the wood gate as though it had burned her.

"Mrs. White, I just walked in." Emma lied. "I called your name but you didn't reply and then I heard something from back here so I thought that maybe you had gone downstairs." Then she realized Mrs. White had asked her why she was early, not what she was doing. "I know I'm early but the coffee shop was crowded and I just wanted a quiet place to sit and maybe do a little studying before work." She added quickly.

Mrs. White looked at her carefully and Emma felt her face flush under Mrs. White's scrutiny.

"You just came in?" Mrs. White asked, her gentle face serious.

Emma nodded her head. "Just a few moments ago."

Mrs. White nodded, seemingly appeased by this answer. "I must not have heard you. I was on the phone in my office. If I'm not in the main room that's where you will usually find me. I never go down there." She informed Emma, looking pointedly at the staircase.

"Oh, okay." Emma said softly, nodding her head in understanding.

"Your shift doesn't start for another thirty minutes so feel free to study or do whatever you need to do until then. I'm just going to be back in my office." Mrs. White said.

Emma smiled at Mrs. White as she walked past her to where she had left her backpack and coffee in the front of the store. She could feel Mrs. White watching her as she walked away but when she looked back as she sat down Mrs. White was walking towards her office. Emma reached into her backpack and pulled out her history book.

What had Mrs. White and Tyler been talking about? She wanted to investigate the staircase some more and find out what was down there but she had a feeling that Mrs. White would be checking on her to make sure Emma was really studying like she said she would be. So Emma opened her history book and began talking notes. Besides, she admitted to herself, she really did need to study.

CHAPTER FIVE

That night Emma stayed up until 2 a.m. doing all the extra homework and studying she had been assigned. She had no idea how she managed to stay awake, normally she was asleep by eleven but the energy that had been pumping through her body all day kept her awake that night as well. When Emma finally brushed her teeth and got ready for bed her mind revisited the mysterious conversation she had overheard that afternoon.

Tyler had seemed completely sane and it was obvious that he and Mrs. White knew each other very well. What was the Circle that Mrs. White had mentioned? And were the objects Mrs. White agreed to protect for him the journals he had been babbling about?

Maybe she should tell Mark what she had overheard. Emma toppled into her bed and slipped under the covers. It was too late to think about this anymore. She had to wake up in five hours and that was going to be a hard enough problem to deal with. School was going to be fun tomorrow.

That night Emma woke with a gasp, her body covered in a cold sweat. Her eyes darted around her room, terrified of the shifting shadows, seeing a room that wasn't there. After a few moments the familiarity of her surroundings began to sink in and she realized that she was safe in her own room. Emma collapsed back into bed, taking in a deep breath to calm herself. Another nightmare.

Energy thrummed through her body. She found herself tapping her fingers uncontrollably on the bed, wondering what time it was and if she could get up yet. Grabbing her clock from the bedside table she jerked it over and held it in front of her face so she could see the time. 5:04. It took a few seconds for that to sink in. 5:04. She felt as energized as if she had slept for half the day but in reality she had only gotten three hours of sleep. *That's not possible.* She thought, shaking her head in disbelief.

Emma slowly sank back down into bed, trying to go back to sleep but it was no use. The nightmare had made her too scared to fall back asleep and her body felt like it was filled with even more energy than it had been yesterday. The buzzing returned to her head with a vengeance, even worse than the day before and Emma couldn't stop her legs from shaking with excess energy. This was ridiculous.

Finally admitting she couldn't stay in bed any longer, which was something she had never thought would happen, Emma swung her legs out from under the sheets and stood up. She stood for a moment trying to decide on her next course of action when her stomach growled loudly. She was starving. Deciding she might as well raid the kitchen since she couldn't sleep Emma snuck downstairs and poured herself a bowl of cereal.

After three bowls of cereal and a banana that had been lying on the counter Emma snuck back upstairs, her hunger temporarily dulled. Emma's energy hadn't abated at all however. Staring longingly at her bed Emma accepted that there was no way she would be able to get back to sleep with this much energy.

Emma looked out her bedroom window. The sky was just beginning to lighten with the approaching dawn. It was light enough to see by though. Turning from the window Emma quickly changed into running shorts and a t-shirt. Normally she hated running but it was the one thing that always drained her of energy.

Grabbing her running shoes and iPod Emma snuck downstairs and put on her shoes at the bottom of the stairway. She paused to grab one of Morgan's running hoodies out of the entry closet. She won't miss it, Emma thought as she zipped it up.

Emma paused and looked up the wooden staircase at the second floor where everyone was sleeping. It was strange to be awake and active before everyone else. Almost surreal even. Emma took a moment to soak in the silence, then she unlocked the front door and walked out.

The morning air was a little chilly but it felt good on Emma's too warm skin. Emma jumped up and down in the front yard to warm up as she unwound her headphones from her iPod. She had just stuck the left one in her ear when she heard a branch snap in the trees across the road from her house. The brush was so thick over there that she couldn't see very far into the woods but she knew that something was out there.

Emma's muscles tensed, ready to sprint back to the house if necessary. The bushes rustled as whatever it was came towards her. Emma was just about to make a run for it when a large furry form burst out of the bushes. Their neighbors giant St. Bernard, Gus, came trotting towards her, a happy canine smile on his face as his tongue curled in the air.

Emma laughed quietly, shaking her head at herself for being so skittish. Gus sat down next to her feet, gazing up at her adoringly. Emma scratched him behind the ears, smiling as he tilted his head into the caress.

"Good morning Gus." She said sweetly. "You're up early, aren't you?"

Gus leaned against her leg and panted happily, his eyes half closed with pleasure as she scratched him behind the ears. Giving him one last pet Emma straightened up and put the other headphone in her ear, turning on her music to something upbeat.

When she finally settled on a good song Emma took off down the road for her early morning run. Just before she ran out of sight a man stepped out of the forest, watching Emma as she ran. When she disappeared around a corner the man looked over at Gus, still sitting happily where Emma had left him. In the blink of an eye the dog disappeared and the man melted back into the forest.

The next week on Thursday afternoon Emma sat in the coffee shop relaxing after school. She had managed to grab one of the smaller plush couches inside with a coffee table in front of it. Propping her feet on the table Emma leaned back and enjoyed her few moments of peace as she snacked on another slice of coffee cake and a ham and cheese croissant.

After Mark helped her with her headaches a week ago and the morning runs she now took every day before school, Emma had the headaches and her excessive energy semi under control. She also suspected Mark had switched her drinks to decaf but she wasn't going to say anything about that. She still only slept about three hours a night but at least she was getting all of her homework done and waking up in time to go run.

64

Emma didn't know what to do about how much she ate. Kathryn had started to comment about how she might have to start going to the grocery store twice a week if Emma kept eating this much. Emma thought that was a little insulting but Kathryn was right, they were running out of food much faster than they used to.

Emma was just finishing the croissant and was contemplating getting some more food when Jason plopped down on the couch next to her.

"Hey Jason." Emma greeted him. She still felt a little on edge around him but she didn't know why. Jason continued to be perfectly friendly to her so she tried not to let on that he made her nervous.

"Hey," He said cheerfully. "I saw you sitting over here by yourself and I thought I would come say hi."

"Oh, okay." Emma said. A slightly awkward pause followed. Emma looked down at her hands that were restlessly tearing apart the small brown bag the pastries came in. Her mind was a complete blank, she couldn't think of anything to say.

"I also had another reason for coming over here." Jason said, breaking the silence.

Emma looked over at him, raising her eyebrows in surprise. "What's the other reason?"

"There is a party this weekend and I was hoping you would go. I could use someone to talk to." Jason said, watching her reaction carefully.

Emma paused thoughtfully. She hadn't gone to a party in a long time, it could be fun.

"Where is it?" She asked.

Jason smiled, looking excited that she was considering it. "It's near Lake Steven, so it's a bit of a drive but I heard the house is awesome. I've been told it's going to be a crazy party."

Emma was interested for a moment, until she realized that he was talking about Chris Miller's party. It was the biggest party of the year that everyone who was considered even semi cool made an appearance to. Emma had never gone.

"You're talking about Chris Miller's party." She laughed, mostly at herself for actually thinking of going to a party.

"Between Morgan and the rest of your friends I think you'll have plenty of people around to talk to." She assured him.

"But none of them are as fun to talk to as you." Jason cajoled. "Come on, it will be fun." He gave her a charming smile. "Amy will be there, and you can even bring your friend Mark with you."

When Emma just shook her head Jason sighed and stood up. "If you change your mind the party is Saturday night. Give me a call if you decide to go."

He began to walk away when he paused and turned back.

"I hope you will change your mind." He murmured before walking away. Emma watched him go, wondering if she dared to show up to the party at all and why he wanted her to.

"A party?!?" Amy squealed over the phone. "I can't believe you're going to go! I've been inviting you to these parties for three years now!"

Emma laughed as she shut her car door and walked towards the garage. She didn't have work that afternoon so she was home early for the first time that week.

"You make it sound like I never go out." Emma said.

"Well…you don't." Amy replied, brutally honest as always.

"I do too!" Emma said indignantly. "I hang out with you all the time."

"Wow, I really am your only friend, aren't I?" Amy teased her. "You have a very sad life."

"Thank you, I really feel the love. Besides I prefer quality over quantity." Emma said with a laugh.

"Very true." Amy agreed and Emma could almost hear her nodding her head. "And because I'm such an amazing friend I will go shopping with you to pick out the perfect outfit for Saturday!"

Emma rolled her eyes. Amy jumped at any possible opportunity to go shopping. It was her favorite thing to do, besides hearing the latest gossip of course.

"I don't know Ayms," Emma said as she walked up to the front door. "It's just a party, why do I need to go shopping?"

"Because I wanted to get a new outfit for myself and now you get to come with me!" Amy informed her. "It will be fun! Please?"

"Do I have a choice?"

"Not really."

"Then I'd love to." Emma said in a falsely sweet voice. "We can go tomorrow after school."

Emma opened the door and heard Morgan yelling in the kitchen. "I've got to go Ayms." She whispered quickly. "I'll talk to you later."

Hanging up the phone Emma wandered over to the kitchen, wondering what had Morgan so upset.

"Why are you making me clean the stupid attic?" Morgan yelled at Steve, who was calmly sitting at the table with the newspaper in front of him.

"Because it needs to be cleaned and you're the only one in this house who doesn't have a real job to keep you busy." Steve replied calmly, turning the page he was reading.

"This is so unfair!" Morgan shrieked. "You're punishing me for having a life!"

When Morgan saw Emma she pointed at her. "Make Emma do it!" She exclaimed. "Emma doesn't have a life and she likes looking through old junk."

Emma glared at Morgan who gave her an evil glare back but Steve ignored their silent exchange, replying calmly. "Emma has a job at the bookstore. And I didn't ask her to do it, I asked you."

"You're so mean!" Morgan shrieked, running out of the kitchen. A few seconds later they heard the door to her room slam shut. Steve sighed and dropped the newspaper onto the table.

"Welcome home Emma." Steve said. "How was your day today?"

Emma shrugged. "Pretty uneventful. Mrs. White didn't need me at work today so I get to have the day off."

"That was nice of her." Steve said, his attention drifting back to the newspaper in front of him.

Emma walked over to the refrigerator and grabbed a soda, as well as snagging a bag of chips from the cupboard. "So why are you making Morgan clean the attic?" Emma asked as she poured ice into a cup for her drink.

"Oh, your mother decided that the attic had to be cleaned this weekend. I'm not sure why but she seems to think it's important." Steve replied absently.

"So Mom told you to clean the attic and you decided to pawn it off on Morgan?" Emma guessed with a smile.

Steve grinned. "I decided that Morgan needed a lesson in responsibility. If that lesson happens to get me out of cleaning the attic…well, that's just an added bonus."

Emma laughed and grabbed her food to head up to her room while Steve returned to reading the paper. When Emma walked into her room she set the food down on her bedside table and grabbed the remote for the small television she had in her room.

She had been missing some of her favorite shows since she had started working in the afternoon and today was the perfect day to get caught up. Luckily she had them all recorded so Emma clicked on the show at the top of the list and got settled in. Grabbing the bag of chips she started munching on them as the show began playing.

"You really have no life, do you?" Morgan said from the doorway.

Emma groaned and dropped her head, reluctantly pausing her show.

"What do you want Morgan?" She asked, wishing Morgan would just cut to the chase and leave her alone.

"I heard you're going to Chris Miller's party this weekend." Morgan said, walking into Emma's room. She shut the door behind her and wandered over to Emma's desk, leaning against it.

"Please come in," Emma muttered under her breath. Morgan pretended not to hear her, instead she looked around Emma's room disdainfully. Emma was instantly aware of how messy her room was. She shifted uncomfortably.

"How do you even know that?" Emma asked as Morgan's gaze landed on the bag of potato chips Emma was eating. Morgan wrinkled her nose with distaste.

"Please, I know everything that goes on at that school." Morgan sneered. "I'm glad Steve was so understanding when he found out you got another Saturday detention." When Emma shifted uncomfortably again Morgan gave her a practiced look of surprise. "You did tell him about that, didn't you? Because I'm a little surprised he would let you go to the party when he told you last week that if you got another detention you would be grounded."

"I was going to tell him." Emma mumbled.

"Really? Why don't you tell him right now? Here, I'll even help you." Morgan said. She opened the door and yelled downstairs. "Dad!"

Emma leaped off her bed. "Morgan! Stop it!" She snapped, grabbing Morgan's arm and pulling her back from the door.

"What's wrong? I thought you were going to tell him." Morgan said snidely.

"I will, I just…" Emma began before she caught herself.

"You just, what? You want to go to the party so you can see Jason and maybe get a chance to talk to him?" Morgan looked Emma up and down, laughing in amusement. "I'd be shocked if he even noticed you were there."

"I never go to parties Morgan, can't you just let me go to this one?" Emma asked, hating the fact that she was almost begging but it was better than letting Morgan get her grounded.

"I'm not the one who made you get detention. You did that all on your own." Morgan pointed out, clearly enjoying making Emma squirm.

"Yes, I know. That was my fault but will you please let it go, just this once?" Emma asked.

"Fine, I won't tell Steve." Morgan said. Emma breathed a sigh of relief. "On one condition." Morgan continued, crossing her arms over her chest.

Emma eyed her warily. "And what would that be?"

"You have to clean out the attic." Morgan replied.

"Seriously Morgan?" Emma stared at her in disbelief. "You're going to make me clean out the attic? Can't you do one thing…" Emma began to argue. Pressure built in her head, threatening to turn into another headache.

"Morgan?" Steve's voice came from downstairs. "Did you call me?"

Morgan raised her eyebrows questioningly at Emma but Emma just glared back at her. With a shrug Morgan opened her mouth to yell back down to Steve.

"Fine!" Emma whispered furiously. "I'll do it."

Morgan grinned. "Sorry Dad," She yelled. "I thought I saw a spider. False alarm."

Turning back to Emma Morgan gave her a smug smile.

"Great! Make sure you get it done tomorrow night while my parents are out having dinner with their friends."

With that she walked out of Emma's room, a triumphant grin on her face. Emma glared after her. Some day she was going to get back at Morgan. Flopping back on the bed Emma looked down at the bag of potato chips that crinkled when she sat down. Remembering Morgan's look of distaste Emma pushed them away angrily and restarted her show.

Emma stood in the laundry room and stared up at the hatch that led to the attic. Emma hated opening this door. She had a fear of things falling on her head, or rather a wise distrust of gravity. Taking a deep breath and steeling her resolve Emma jumped, her fingers grasping at the string connected to the door. The door was surprisingly heavy and not very willing to open.

Using her weight Emma managed to get the hatch to slowly swing down. Grabbing the ladder that was attached to the inside of the hatch door she slowly pulled that down also until it rested on the floor. Emma sneezed as dust swirled down from the attic. No one had been up there in years.

The house was dead silent as Emma climbed up the ladder into the attic. Kathryn and Steve were having dinner over at a friend's house, like they did every Friday night. Morgan was out with friends somewhere. Emma hadn't asked where and Morgan hadn't volunteered the information.

Usually Emma liked having the house to herself but for some reason the idea of going into the attic with no one else around wasn't very appealing. Luckily Kathryn's standards for cleaning the attic weren't very high. She just wanted it dusted and the boxes arranged against one side of the wall.

Crawling into the attic Emma stood up and pulled the string to turn on the single light bulb in the sloped room. Emma was surprised by how spacious the room was, despite being filled with boxes. Aside from the dust it didn't look like how Emma imagined it would.

Emma always pictured a room filled with old pieces of furniture and broken bicycles, maybe even a creepy doll propped up in a rocking chair. Instead there was just a lot of dust and neatly packed boxes. Deciding that the faster she cleaned the faster she would be done, Emma climbed back down the ladder to grab the cleaning supplies.

An hour and a lot of sneezing later Emma finally finished dusting the room. Now she just had to organize the boxes and stack them against the far wall. Most of the boxes were already labeled. Kathryn was both an organization and a cleaning freak, which was probably why she had the sudden urge to clean the attic. All the labels were typed and neatly taped on the boxes. Morgan's baby clothes, wedding photo albums, childhood photo albums, old clothes, the usual things one would expect to find in an attic if they weren't looking for creepy dolls.

Emma was almost done stacking the boxes against the far wall when she noticed one box in the far corner of the attic. The light barely reached back there, she must have just over looked it earlier. Emma walked over, careful not to hit her head on the sloping roof. She had to get down on her hands and knees but she managed to grab the box and drag it to the middle of the room directly under the light bulb so she could see it better.

There was no label on the side of the box. This box seemed different somehow, older maybe. Definitely more beat up, but it still managed to hold itself together. Curious about what was inside Emma opened the box. The first thing she saw was a neatly folded blue and white-checkered baby blanket.

Emma carefully picked it up and held it in her hands. Something about it seemed familiar, like it was part of a memory she couldn't quite recall. Then a picture frame caught her eye and she carefully set the blanket on the floor. Emma picked up the picture and stared at it. In the picture was a young couple holding a baby that was wrapped in the blue and white blanket. They looked so young, maybe around twenty years old, but they were happy. In the photo the man stood behind the woman with his arms around her as she held the baby. They were looking down at the sleeping infant and it was easy to see how much they loved the child.

Suddenly it was very important for Emma to know who that couple was. Opening the back of the frame Emma pulled out the photo to see if there was anything written on the back. In the bottom corner in cursive was written *The Forgeron Family*. Emma's hands started shaking. The Forgeron family.

That name, she knew it from somewhere. Emma frowned. Everything in this box seemed familiar, like she should know where it all came from but the memories were just out of reach. Now as she turned the picture over in her hand she wondered if Kathryn knew this box was here and where it had come from. Emma lightly touched the smiling faces of the couple. She wished she could have known them.

Carefully putting the photo back in the picture frame Emma gently placed it on top of the blanket and looked to see what else there was in the box. Only three other things were in the box. A small wooden box, an old leather journal, and a few newspaper clippings.

Emma picked up the small wooden box next, holding it in the palm of her hand. The box was plain, nothing out of the ordinary. Emma probably wouldn't have looked at it twice if she had seen it lying around the house. Gently opening it Emma found an old bracelet inside.

The bracelet was made of leather, three strands woven together with flat metal disks evenly spaced throughout the design. The metal disks gleamed in the dim light of the attic, somehow capturing the light and drawing it in. It looked like one disk was missing though. There was a gap in the design. Emma traced a finger over one of the metal disks.

She quickly pulled her hand back when she felt a strange sensation pass from the bracelet to her finger. In the middle of the metal disk she had touched a black dot appeared. Emma blinked in

72

astonishment as the black dot elongated and twisted across the surface until it had formed into a symbol much like the one on the metal disk Tyler had given her.

Quickly she rubbed the other two disks, watching wide-eyed as symbols appeared on their surfaces as well. For a moment Emma stared at the bracelet, not sure what the symbols meant or what to do with it now. Emma grabbed the box she found the bracelet in and looked to see if there was anything else in there, anything that might explain what she had just seen but the box was empty. Maybe the journal said something about it though. Eyeing the bracelet suspiciously, she replaced it in the box and placed the box on the blanket with the photo.

Emma picked up the journal and studied it carefully, hoping there weren't going to be any nasty surprises if she opened it. Hard backed brown leather, intricate designs were etched into the cover and along the seam, similar to the ones on the bracelet but subtly different.

When Emma opened it the first thing she noticed was how nice the paper was. High quality, soft, this wasn't factory made and bulk ordered. Emma didn't know if she had ever seen anything like it. On the inside written in the same cursive as on the back of the photo was written *Alexandra Savage.* Her mother. Emma's jaw dropped when she realized she was opening her mother's journal. She had wished for years that she had something of her parents. Now she finally did.

Emma eagerly opened to the first page and began reading.

June 25, 1988
Dear Diary,
I feel a little bit silly saying that, like I am eight years old and writing to my imaginary best friend. I guess most people would still consider me a child, I'm only fourteen. The past few weeks have made me feel much older though, and the things I've seen…no fourteen year old should have to deal with these things.

Writing in a journal was the grief counselor's idea, he thinks that writing down our feelings will help my brothers and I cope with what happened. As if writing about it would make things better. I think he's an idiot.

The Blade thought it was a good idea though so he went out and bought journals for us. I think he was just trying to think of something to do to help. Drake threw his in the fire as soon as The Blade handed it to him. The Blade should have seen that one coming. Drake doesn't have emotions anymore, just anger. The Blade didn't seem to care that Drake threw his away. I thought that was strange until I passed his room later I saw he had pulled out his throwing knives and was drawing a target on the front of his journal. I don't think he's going to be pouring his heart out into a journal either.

I was going to follow Drake's example and do something dramatic like throw mine in the lake but when The Blade handed it to me he looked at me with those sad, solemn eyes of his and said, "Please, just try." I couldn't stand seeing the sadness in his eyes so I caved and took the journal. He actually managed to look happy for a moment, which in a way makes this worth it.

My brothers and I didn't used to be so bad at talking about our feelings. Well, Drake was but that's just who he is. The Blade used to be much more open though. Ever since what happened, we've all just kind of withdrew from each other. At first I tried to get the others to talk but after a while it was just easier to shut everyone else out too. I guess the reality of what happened finally sank in. In my better moments I worry about my brothers, I hope they are doing okay. I can never bring myself to ask them though. I guess I'm scared they'll ask me the same question and I won't know what to say.

Emma sat in the quiet attic and stared down at the journal in her hands. Alexandra had sounded so sad. Emma placed the journal on the blanket with the other things. Reaching into the box Emma pulled out the newspaper clippings. It was just a few articles about a car crash with a picture of the car. Apparently it had been hit by a semi and spun off into a lake. No bodies had been found but the passengers were presumed dead.

There were also a few articles from 1988 about the mysterious killing of Richard and Kate Savage. It mentioned the family fortune had been divided between their three children with the oldest son being given controlling interest in the family's company. Emma wasn't sure what those articles had to do with anything but she placed them back in the box and repacked everything else. She didn't know how the box had ended up in the attic or if it actually had belonged to her mother but Emma was taking it to her room.

After some careful maneuvering Emma managed to get the box down the ladder without dropping it or falling down herself, a feat she was a little surprised she accomplished. Emma glanced at the clock. 9:50. Kathryn and Steve would be home soon.

Grabbing the box she hurried to her room and hid it in the back of her closet. She didn't know why but a small voice in the back of her head warned her not to let anyone see her with the box. Going back to the attic Emma took one last look around to make sure it was clean, then she turned off the light and climbed down.

Just as she was closing up the hatch she heard Steve and Kathryn pull into the garage. Emma ran to her room and quickly changed out of her dusty cleaning clothes and into a pair of comfy sweats and a t-shirt. If Kathryn and Steve found out that Emma had cleaned the attic and not Morgan then both she and Morgan would be in big trouble. Emma stuffed the dusty clothes into her hamper and jumped on her bed, turning on her television just as she heard Steve yell.

"Hello? Anyone home?"

"In here!" Emma yelled back.

Emma heard footsteps approach her door, then the door opened and Steve stuck his head into her room.

"You alive?" He asked.

"Yeah," Emma replied. "It was touch and go for a while but I managed to pull through."

I'm glad you survived." Steve said with a warm smile. "Do you know where Morgan is?"

Emma shrugged, looking uninterested. "Do I ever know where Morgan is?"

Steve chuckled. "Good point. Alright, I'll leave you alone now." Steve started closing the door but then he hesitated. Sticking his head back into the room he looked at her as though he was choosing his words carefully. "You know Emma, maybe you should go out sometime. You only go through high school once, you should enjoy it."

Emma laughed. "Is this your way of telling me to get a life?"

Steve shrugged. "There are worse things you could do."

"I actually have plans to go out tomorrow night." Emma informed him. "And not just with Amy either." She added when Steve looked skeptical.

"Oh really? And what are these big plans?" Steve asked, an amused smile on his face.

"I was invited to a party tomorrow night." Emma said carefully, watching Steve's face for any hint of disapproval.

Steve raised an eyebrow. "A party, huh?" He narrowed his eyes at her but Emma kept an innocent expression on her face. "All right, but don't do anything stupid." He warned.

Emma gave him a mischievous smile. "Me? Do something stupid? Never!"

"Hmph." Steve grunted, but he was smiling as he shut her door.

Emma smiled to herself as she thought about seeing Jason at the party tomorrow night. Despite the nagging sense of uncertainty she couldn't deny that the idea of seeing him excited her. It was frustrating wanting to be near someone but feeling so nervous around them that she just wanted to run away.

Her thoughts turned to the box of things she had found in the attic and she looked over at her closet. She had no idea why the box had been hidden in the attic but she wasn't going to tell Kathryn or Steve that she had found it.

Remembering the bracelet she had found Emma rolled off her bed and hurried over to the closet. Digging through the box she pulled out the bracelet. The symbols still showed clearly on the surface of the metal. Emma pushed herself to her feet and walked over to her desk where she had placed the metal disk Tyler had given her. Emma picked up the loose disk in her right hand, surprised when the metal felt warm to the touch. She was always cold in her room, she wasn't sure how the metal had gotten so warm.

Emma held the disk and the bracelet side by side. Sure enough, the loose disk matched the other three in the bracelet. There was one empty spot where the loose disk could fit into but

Emma didn't see any way to put them together. On a whim Emma pressed the disk into the empty spot. Light flashed, bright enough to blind her.

Emma dropped the bracelet, pressing the palm of her hands into her eyes. She heard a roaring sound in her ears and swayed on her feet as a major head rush hit her. Emma clutched the back of her desk chair in one hand to keep from falling over. In a moment the dizzy sensation passed and Emma could see again.

The bracelet wasn't on the desk, it must have fallen onto the floor when she dropped it. Grumbling in annoyance Emma got down on her hands and knees to search under her desk. Whatever that flash of light had been she hoped it wasn't going to happen again. Pressing her cheek to the floor she could just barely see the bracelet under the side drawers of the desk.

Emma reached her right hand into the space, having to flatten herself against the floor to slide her hand underneath. She felt the tips of her finger barely brush the bracelet. Emma grunted and scooted herself a little closer. She just managed to hook her middle finger over the bracelet to tug it closer to her.

Just as she tried to pull it out she felt something slither over her hand and circle around her wrist. Emma yelped and yanked her arm out from underneath the desk, clawing at whatever had latched onto her wrist with her left hand before she even saw what it was.

The bracelet hung from her wrist, innocently gleaming in her bedroom light. Emma panted in panic, her pulse racing. For a terrifying moment she had thought that some impossible creature like a fairy had latched onto her. Emma tugged at the bracelet, trying to figure out how to take it off but there was no clasp, no opening of any sort.

She tried rolling it off her wrist but it wouldn't fit over her hand no matter how hard she tugged at it. Emma kept yanking at the bracelet, beginning to panic when she realized she couldn't get it off. She pulled and clawed until her wrist was sore and throbbing. Then she grabbed a pair of scissors from her desk and tried cutting it off but the scissors didn't even make a mark on the leather.

Next she grabbed a knife and tried sawing it off, but with no better results. It was as though the bracelet was made of titanium. Emma briefly considered breaking into an auto shop for a blowtorch before dismissing the idea. She wasn't accurate enough with her left hand for a stunt like that.

Emma flopped back on her bed with a grunt, holding her wrist above her head to stare at the bracelet.

"What *are* you?!?" She muttered at it.

The bracelet didn't respond and Emma rolled her eyes, dropping her arm back onto the bed. She would have to deal with it later. She was tired and she had a party to get ready for tomorrow.

CHAPTER SIX

Chris Miller's family owned a log lodge on Stevens Lake thirty miles from town. Every year his parents attended a business conference and left Chris home alone. So every year Christ threw the biggest, craziest party of the school year. As Mark drove up to the house Emma looked out the window at all the students piling out of their cars. She had a feeling that Chris had outdone himself this year.

Emma could hear the music bursting out of the windows and open doors from half a mile away, accompanied by the yells and screams of half the student population. Emma's courage deserted her as soon as she saw the crowds of people gathered around on the front lawn of the house.

More and more spilled out of the doorway every second. If it had just been her she would have turned around and driven home but Mark and Amy were expecting her to stay. And, a treacherous part of her mind whispered, somewhere in there Jason was looking for her too.

Mark hit the brakes, swearing under his breath as a group of guys ran out into the road right in front of his truck. The headlights of Mark's truck were like a spotlight for their childish antics as they jumped around, wrestling with each other as they crossed the road toward the party.

Emma looked at Mark's face, wondering what his reaction to all this would be. He didn't go to things like this. As far as she knew Mark didn't really have any other friends besides for her. He was just a quiet guy who liked to keep to himself. Mark shook his shaggy brown hair out of his face, then he pushed up his glasses that had slipped down his nose. He looked tense and annoyed, but that might have had something to do with the complete lack of parking spots available and how many times people had jumped out in front of his car.

"I should have just hit them." Mark muttered, as the guys wrestled their way across the road.

Emma grinned but didn't say anything. He slowly began driving forward again, not even bothering to turn into Chris's long driveway. All the cars parked along the street were a pretty good indicator that there was no chance of getting a spot next to the house.

Emma looked down at her lap, suddenly feeling nervous. This had been a stupid idea. She wasn't friends with these people. These were Morgan's friends, the ones who stared at her as she walked by and whispered when her back was turned. At best they didn't even know she existed, at worst they probably thought she was a freak just like Morgan said she was.

Emma tugged at the skirt she was wearing, already regretting letting Amy talk her into buying it yesterday. It was cream colored, mid-thigh length with layers that flared out when she spun. Amy had coaxed her into buying it when Emma had been excited about going to the party and loved the idea of looking pretty. Now she felt defensive and would have given anything to be in a good pair of jeans. Or even better to be back home in her comfy sweats. Emma pressed a hand against her temple, hoping to relieve some of the pressure in her head.

"Finally, a place to park!" Mark said suddenly, breaking the silence in the car. Emma jumped a little, looking up from her lap to see where they were. Mark had pulled into the field across from Chris' house with a bunch of other cars and parked next to a bright red jeep. Only trucks, jeeps and hummers were able to jump the curb, anyone driving a smaller car had to keep driving until they found an open spot on the side of the road.

Mark jumped out of his car, a smug smile on his face.

"I love this truck." He said, grinning back at Emma who was still sitting in the cab of the truck. "Well, come on!" Mark exclaimed. "Let's go."

Emma reluctantly opened her door, holding her skirt down with one hand as she awkwardly jumped out of the truck. Luckily she wasn't wearing heels or Mark would have had to carry her across the field. She was accident prone at the best of times, in heels she was a walking catastrophe. And that was on level surfaces. Mark waited patiently as Emma straightened her outfit and gathered her courage before joining him on the other side of the truck.

"Are you sure you want to go to this party?" Mark asked when she walked up to him. He ducked his head to get a better look at her face. "We can just go home if you want."

Emma smiled at him reassuringly. "We're already here, we might as well go inside. Besides, Amy will be upset if I don't at least make an appearance after she spent so much time coordinating my outfit." Emma said with an exaggerated wave at her skirt.

Mark slung an arm around Emma's shoulders in a brotherly fashion. The top of Emma's head barely reached his shoulder and his arm was so heavy it almost knocked her off balance. A small part of her brain pointed out that his arm felt a lot heavier than it should have. "It would be a shame not to let people admire you when you look so beautiful." He said, giving her a slight squeeze.

"You are such a liar." Emma laughed. She craned her neck to look up at Mark. "You know, I never realized how absolutely tiny I am next to you. You're huge."

Mark gently pushed her away, laughing as she almost tripped on her own feet before he reached out and steadied her with a hand under her elbow. "Really? Because I realize it all the time. You're like a little munchkin. Or an adorable puppy that trips over itself." He said, pinching her cheek.

Emma swatted his hand away. "Careful, puppies bite." She warned. Emma paused. "Munchkins do too, now that I think about it." She added thoughtfully.

"I would like to see you try." Mark said with a grin. Emma wisely chose not to accept that challenge and instead started walking towards the house.

Amy was waiting outside for them as they approached the party. She was talking to a few of the guys on the wrestling team but when she saw Emma, Amy raced over and nearly tackled her in an enthusiastic hug.

"I can't believe you're here!" She exclaimed. "I'm so glad you came! We're going to have so much fun tonight!"

Emma laughed at Amy's exuberance and felt herself relax a little. As long as she stuck around Amy she would be fine.

"You look great by the way!" Amy said, yelling a little to be heard over the music and the crowds. "I told you the skirt would be perfect! Come inside, we'll get you a drink!"

Amy grabbed Emma's hand and pulled her towards the house. Emma cast a helpless look over her shoulder at Mark but he just shrugged and followed the two girls as they pushed through the crowd. Inside, girls stood huddled together in tight circles talking and laughing while guys played video games and did stupid stunts. Red cups were everywhere, covering tables, knocked over on the floor, stacked on the stairway. Some were even in people's hands. Everyone was packed so tightly together that it was impossible to move without running into someone.

As they made their way through the crowd kids from their school stared at Emma, obviously surprised to see her there. Amy's grip on Emma's hand became a lifeline that she clung to as they moved closer towards the kitchen.

Amy smiled at her over her shoulder as she squeezed past a group of girls who were staring at Emma, showing expressions ranging from confusion and disbelief to annoyance. Emma half-heartedly returned Amy's smile before looking over her own shoulder for Mark. Luckily he was head and shoulders taller than most people in the room so he was easy to spot. That reassured Emma a little bit as Amy kept leading her further into the house.

In the kitchen there were four large red water coolers on the counters and the kitchen table was covered with bags of red cups. Groups of people surrounded all of the water coolers, everyone shoving their cups forward so that they could get a drink first.

"You want a drink?" Amy shouted above the crowd, pausing by the kitchen.

Emma shook her head. "No, I'm good."

Amy laughed and pulled Emma towards one of the water coolers anyways. "Trust me, if you don't want to spend half the night telling people you don't want a drink then you should always be holding one in your hand. You don't have to drink it if you don't want to."

Snagging two cups from the table Amy smiled flirtatiously at a big football player standing by one of the coolers. The football player straightened up and immediately pushed the crowd back so she could slip in and fill the cups with what looked like red Kool-Aid.

"Thanks!" Amy said, smiling sweetly at him.

"No problem." The guy replied, giving her a wink.

Returning to Emma, Amy handed her one of the drinks then smoothly turned to lean against the kitchen counter and take a sip of her own. Emma raised an eyebrow at her.

"Nicely done." Emma smirked.

Amy tossed her long blonde curls over one shoulder and grinned at Emma. "And you think being a flirt is a bad thing." She said playfully.

Emma rolled her eyes at Amy but couldn't stop herself from smiling. Looking around the room Emma was amazed at how many people were there. As she scanned the crowd a pair of bright blue eyes locked with hers. Loraine smiled mockingly from across the room, tipping her cup towards Emma in a sarcastic salute.

Feeling suddenly overwhelmed by the crowd pressing in around her Emma desperately looked around for an escape. Across the living room packed with teenagers was a door leading out to the back porch. Emma leaned towards Amy and yelled, "I'm going outside for a few minutes to get some fresh air. I'll be back soon!"

Amy nodded. "Do you want me to go with you?" She yelled back.

"No, it's fine. You have fun here." Emma said.

She waved at Amy and turned to merge into the crowd that was gathered in the living room. Within seconds Emma was disoriented. Music pounded in her ears, fighting to be heard over the shouts and yells of all the kids there. It was so loud Emma had a difficult time thinking. The music just filled all the space in her head until there was no room for anything else.

Bodies shifted and moved around her, bumping into her and stumbling into her path so she had to constantly be on guard for stray hands or elbows that might hit her, or worse, her drink. Finally she saw a gap to the door open in the crush of bodies. Emma dove forward, squeezing her way through just as someone shifted to close the gap. Emma's hand landed on the door handle and with a victorious smile she opened the door and slipped out onto the porch.

The twilight breeze rushed into the house past her as she stepped outside. The wind felt cool on her warm cheeks, a welcome relief from the cloying warmth of the house. Emma took a deep breath, allowing the cool breeze rush into her lungs. The suffocating feeling she had been battling eased a bit with each breath she took of the cool fresh air. She had only been outside for a few seconds and she could already feel herself relaxing.

The porch was a wide expanse of space that stretched the length of the back of the house. The lodge was built on a hill so the first floor was actually the top floor and the bottom floor was built into the ground. Plastic lawn chairs littered the porch for the guests to sit on.

Emma wasn't the only one who seemed to have a hard time with the crowd and the noise. A few couples leaned against the porch railing, cuddling as they looked out over the romantic scene. Groups of friends stood in circles where they could find space on the porch as they talked and laughed.

Emma found an open spot along the railing to lean against, and wandered over to it. She placed her drink on the rough wood and propped her elbows on either side of it as she dropped her chin into the palm of her hand and stared out at the lake pensively. It was a beautiful view from the porch and Emma sighed appreciatively as she soaked in the scenery.

Pine trees framed the sides of the backyard, casting a beautiful border of the view with deep sweeping branches that swayed in the breeze. A thin strip of smooth pebbles separated the emerald green grass of the backyard from the dark smooth surface of the lake. The water was so still it looked like glass as it reflected the moon and the stars. For one moment the noise of the party faded away and it was just Emma, the lake, and the breeze that connected them.

84

A large hand grabbed Emma's shoulder and she bit back a scream, whirling around to see who it was.

"Emma!" Jason exclaimed, pulling her into a big bear hug. "You came! I didn't think you would. You never called me."

Emma's stomach lodged itself somewhere in her throat as she returned his hug. "Yeah, well, I didn't really have anything else going on tonight." She said distractedly. Crushed against his chest like she was, she could smell the musky but slightly sweet scent of Jason's cologne. Sparks began going off in her stomach and she quickly put her hands on his chest to gently ease out of his hug.

Emma wished she didn't react so badly to his presence, the butterflies and the shocks to her system were hard enough to handle. Knowing that she felt like this for the guy Morgan was trying to date was even worse though. As Emma looked into his smiling face she couldn't help but wish that she was the one he was involved with, not Morgan. Except there was that inexplicable sense that there was something different about him, something she didn't know and that made it hard to relax around him.

"As flattering as your reason is, I'm still glad you're here." Jason said drily. "Are you okay? You look like you just saw a ghost or something." He asked, bending down so he could see her face more clearly.

"Oh, yeah I'm fine." Emma said, shifting away from his probing gaze. She looked away, not wanting to make eye contact with him. She wasn't a very good liar.

Jason leaned against the railing next to her and took a sip out of a water bottle he was holding. Emma gave him a cheeky look and nudged him playfully with her shoulder.

"Where'd you get that?" She teased him.

Jason tilted the water bottle in his hands and looked down at it. Glancing at Emma out of the corner of his eye, his lips quirked in a crooked smile.

"I snuck it in." He confessed.

Emma's bangs slipped over her eyes and she blew them back with an irritated exhalation. "I wish I had thought of that."

"Really?" Jason raised his eyebrows in surprise, looking down at the cup in Emma's hand.

She lifted it in a silent toast, her lips twisting in a wry smile. "Amy." She said simply.

"Ahh." Jason nodded knowingly.

They stood silently for a moment, both leaning against the railing looking out at the lake. Emma snuck a glance at him out of the corner of her eye. He looked good tonight, dressed in a sharp white button up shirt with the sleeves rolled up and pushed past his elbows. The white shirt contrasted with his dark blue jeans and dark leather belt. Effortlessly handsome.

Emma sighed and looked down at the rough wood of the railing. She had no idea how to talk to a guy like him. Emma scrambled to think of something to say that would ease the awkwardness she felt.

"It's crazy in there!" Emma said, motioning towards the house. She could still hear the music and the voices of the people inside but the walls were enough of a barrier that the noise was just a distant roar.

"Yeah." Jason agreed, looking back over his shoulder at the house. "Morgan loves the crowds and the noise but I don't really like it. There's too much going on, it's overwhelming."

Emma propped her elbows on the railing next to him and they were silent, staring out and the lake. As she stared out at the magical scene with this strange boy next to her she thought of the fairies and the strange bracelet. Maybe if those existed there were other magical things in this world. Like maybe the lake was a portal to someplace far far away and if she just jumped into it she could just disappear to somewhere else. Maybe someplace where her parents hadn't died and she didn't see strange things. Where she could date guys like Jason and have a group of girl friends that she could hang out at parties with. It was a nice dream.

Inside the house Mark slouched against the wall, arms crossed and a scowl on his face. He hated this party. A girl sprinted in front of Mark squealing in laughter. Chasing after her a skater guy with shaggy hair and a baseball hat pulled low over his face vaulted over the couch next to Mark. He missed his landing though and stumbled, his shoulder ramming into Mark's side. Mark growled and shoved the guy off of him as the girl laughed and taunted the boy before running off again.

86

"Sorry, dude!" The skater boy yelled, not even bothering to look at Mark as he chased after the girl again.

Mark grunted in annoyance. The idea of taking Emma to a party to distract her from all the crazy things that had been happening lately had sounded so good yesterday when she had told him about it. Now it seemed like a stupid idea. A very stupid idea. Mark snarled at another guy who backed up into him, startling the guy and the girl he was with. They both quickly walked away.

Mark straightened up from the wall. He was ready to leave, and if that meant grabbing Emma and throwing her over his shoulder he would. Mark looked around, trying to find Emma in the crowd but he couldn't see her anywhere.

Mark frowned, battling the urge to shove everyone out of his way until he found her. He didn't like her being out of his sight in a place like this. Finally he spotted Amy standing in the kitchen talking to some guy. Amy would know where Emma was. Mark pushed away from the wall and strode through the crowd.

"Whoa, careful there." Amy said with a laugh when someone bumped the football player, Vince, and he stumbled into her, pinning her against the kitchen counter. She put her hands on his chest to gently push him away but he didn't move back, instead he shifted even closer towards her, his hands moving to her hips.

"Maybe I like it here." Vince said with a leer, flexing his fingers and leaning into her.

Amy pushed against his chest harder but he only pulled her tighter against him. "Vince, stop." She snapped. "Get off me." Amy pushed at his hands, trying to get him to let go but Vince only laughed.

"Oh come on, don't play hard to get when we both know you want me." He said, leaning in to kiss her.

Amy pushed against his chest again as hard as she could, turning her face away. "I said no! Get off!" She struggled to get away but he wouldn't let her go.

"Hey!" Mark yelled, brushing past Loraine to grab Vince's shoulder. "She said no. Get off her."

Vince pushed Mark away with one arm, not even bothering to turn away from Amy. "Go away, this has nothing to do with you."

Mark grabbed Vince by the shoulder again. "I told you to let her go." He growled.

Vince spun around, slamming his right fist into Mark's jaw in a vicious right hook. A loud crack split the air and Mark tumbled to the floor, right at Loraine's feet. Vince cursed, cradling his right hand against his chest. The cracking sound had been his hand.

Around them everyone turned to stare and dead silence fell in the room. For a moment everyone was shocked silent, then yells of a fight began to race through the house. Within seconds a circle had formed around Mark and Vince as everyone packed closer to see what would happen. They were all trying to see what poor guy had gotten into a fight with Vince. Mark propped himself up on his elbows and Loraine looked down at him with a smirk.

"Are you really going to let him hit you like that?" She asked, her voice so soft only Mark could hear. "You and I both know you could take him with one hand tied behind your back. Why don't you show everyone what you can do for once?"

Mark scowled at Loraine and pushed himself to his feet. "Shut up." He hissed, turning his back on her. The crowd cheered when Mark stood up, and bets started being shouted out on how badly Vince would beat Mark. Mark ignored them though, his entire focus centered on Vince where he stood in the kitchen still cradling his right hand.

"Yeah, you're a real man." Mark mocked him, staring at Vince with contempt. "Forcing yourself on a girl, using surprise to land a punch on some nerd. You must be feeling so manly right now."

"Shut up!" Vince yelled at him, grabbing Mark by the collar of his shirt.

"Or what? You're going to hit me again?" Mark asked.

Vince hesitated for a moment but the yelling of the crowd hardened. "Yeah, that sounds like a great idea." He said as he drew his arm back to punch Mark again.

Out on the deck Jason shifted to face Emma. She could feel his gaze on her face as she looked out at the lake and nervous butterflies twisted in her stomach. She glanced at him out of the corner of her eye and raised an eyebrow at him.

88

"You're missing the view." She murmured.

"I don't think I am." He replied. A light breeze blew a strand of hair across Emma's face and Jason reached a hand out to tuck the strand behind her ear. Emma slowly turned to face him. He was leaning towards her, bright blue eyes fixed on hers with one arm leaning against the railing.

The moment stretched, heightening as they stared into each others eyes. Then a laugh burst out of Emma and she covered her mouth with a hand, the corners of her eyes crinkling as she looked at him.

"I'm sorry." She gasped, trying not to laugh again. "That was sweet, really."

Jason gave her a crooked smile and shook his head slightly.

"There's something about you. You're different from other girls." He murmured.

Emma froze. Flashes of all the things she had thought she had seen and all the things that made her crazy flashed through her head. He couldn't possibly know about all those things, and yet she had the irrational fear that he could look inside her head and hear what she was thinking right now.

"Different?" Her voice broke slightly on the word. Emma coughed to cover it up and stood up so she wasn't leaning on the railing anymore. "How so?"

Jason's brow furrowed as he looked at her and he slowly stood up too. He opened his mouth to say something when yells about a fight floated out onto the porch. Emma's head whipped around. She craned her neck to look inside the house, suddenly worried. She had a bad feeling one of her friends was involved. Emma hurried towards the door but Jason halted her with a hand on her arm.

"Where are you going?" He asked, holding her back. "You shouldn't go in there, you could get hurt."

Emma shook off his restraining hand. "I have to find Mark and Amy."

She ran into the house, pushing through the crowd. Bodies were packed tight, everyone staring over at the kitchen. Emma squeezed her way through the crowd, sensing Jason right behind her. She kept looking for Mark but she didn't see him anywhere.

She was getting closer to the kitchen where the fight was happening.

She heard people yelling out encouragement to Vince to punch somebody. Emma paused, turning her back to the kitchen so she could get a better look at the faces in the crowd. She didn't much care about the fight, finding Mark was her main concern. Jason pushed through the crowd to stand next to her, a little disheveled from his struggle to get through.

"You see him?" Emma yelled.

Jason shook his head, opening his mouth to reply but Emma had already moved on. She was just about to go look for Mark in another room when over the noise of the crowd she heard Amy scream, "Mark!" Emma whipped her head around, looking to where the scream had come from. Amy's voice had come from the kitchen.

"Oh no." Emma groaned. She made a beeline towards the kitchen, shoving her way through the crowd when it got too thick. Finally she burst through the crush of bodies just in time to see Vince punch Mark in the face. Mark stumbled backwards, trying to dodge the blow but it didn't work. The punch skimmed his jaw just enough to send him sprawling on the floor. Emma jumped forward to help him but Jason caught her mid-air, wrapping an arm around her waist and swinging her around to place her behind him. Momentarily disoriented, Emma looked up into Jason's determined eyes.

"Stay!" He ordered, glaring at her.

Emma gaped at him, too shocked to respond. Satisfied she would stay Jason turned and ran into the kitchen. Emma saw Vince land a kick to Mark's ribs before Jason grabbed him and pushed him away.

"Vince, stop! What the hell are you doing?" Jason yelled at him, putting himself in between Mark and Vince. He kept both of his hands on Vince's chest, pushing him back as the bigger boy tried to charge forward.

"Get off me!" Vince snapped, practically frothing at the mouth in anger. He tried to push Jason to the side and dodge around him but Jason stayed directly in front of Vince no matter what he did. With a loud roar Vince took a wild swing at Jason.

90

Jason easily ducked it, coming back up with an upper cut to Vince's stomach that made Vince double over, gasping for breath.

Amy and Emma exchanged wide-eyed looks from across the kitchen. Remembering Mark at the same time they rushed over to him, bending down to help him to his feet.

"Mark! Are you okay?" Emma asked, kneeling down next to him on the hard kitchen floor. Mark nodded, lips pressed in a thin line as Emma pulled his arm around her shoulders so she could help him up.

Mark groaned as he stood and held his ribs where Vince had kicked him. "Yeah, I think I'm fine." His voice was terse when he replied. Emma exchanged a worried look with Amy who was supporting him on his other side.

"Emma, take him outside." Jason called over his shoulder, keeping himself between Vince and Mark. Vince straightened up, sucking in a deep breath of air. His face was bright red and he had a wild look in his eyes as his gaze fixated on Jason. "I'll be out in a few minutes."

Emma and Amy each ducked under one of Mark's arms and led him through the crowd and out the front door. The front yard of the lodge was a landscape artists dream. Down the front steps of the house a path of light grey pebbles led across the yard to circle around a beautiful water fountain. A small path split off from the main one to curve to the right where there was a pristine rose garden. Another path split off to the left to lead over to a koi pond underneath a weeping willow tree. At the base of the tree was a small stone bench for anyone who wished to sit as they watched the fish. Emma caught Amy's eye and gestured at the bench with her head. Amy nodded and the two girls led Mark over to the bench to sit down.

Once they got him settled Emma immediately knelt on the ground next to him so she could get a better look at his face.

"Mark, what happened? How did you get in a fight with Vince?" Emma asked. She gently placed a hand on his jaw, tilting his head to catch the light from the front of the house so she could get a better look at where he had been hit. Mark winced and took a breath but Amy spoke first.

"Mark was trying to help me." Amy's voice was tight with restrained fury. Shocked, Emma looked up from her examination of Mark's jaw to stare at her. Amy's eyes blazed in anger and her hands were balled into fists, so tight that her knuckles had turned white. "Vince kept grabbing me, he wouldn't let go. I tried to push him off but he just laughed. Mark ran over to help me and that's when Vince hit him."

"Vince grabbed you?" Emma repeated, shocked. Her face clouded in anger. "That son of a…"

"Emma!" Jason called as he jogged over. "Is Mark okay?"

Jason's white shirt was disheveled, the sleeve on his right arm had unrolled and now brushed his hand. She thought she saw a trace of red on his hand but Jason quickly tucked his hand into his pocket before she could tell for sure. She looked up at his face and noticed that his cheeks were red and his hair was a mess as well.

"I'm fine." Mark bit out, glaring at Jason.

"I think he's okay." Emma answered, slowly standing up so she could talk to him. Amy sat down on the stone bench next to Mark. She began probing at his ribs but Mark brushed her hands away.

"I grabbed an icepack for you." Jason said, handing the icepack to Mark. "I figured your eye might need it, or maybe your ribs."

He looked closer at Mark's face while Mark stared back at him. Jason's eyes widened slightly in shock.

"Wow, not even a bloody lip." Jason commented. "That's surprising, Vince never holds back when he throws a punch."

Mark shrugged and looked down. "Maybe he didn't think he needed to hit as hard as usual."

Jason gave Mark a hard stare which he returned with one of his own. Emma glanced back and forth between them, feeling like she missed something. Amy looked back and forth between them as well, then looked at Emma and shrugged.

"Yeah." Jason said slowly, dropping Mark's stare. "Maybe that's it."

Turning towards Emma he lightly touched her elbow as Amy began fussing over Mark.

"You should probably take Mark home now." Jason murmured, his gaze flitting to the house then back to her.

"Okay." Emma whispered.

Emma blew out a breath as Jason walked away, then turned to look back at Mark.

"Okay tough guy." She said, holding her hand out to help him up. "Let's get you home."

CHAPTER SEVEN

Emma and Mark were quiet as she drove his truck back to town, both preoccupied with their own thoughts. Emma kept glancing down at the bracelet on her wrist, trying again and again to come up with a logical explanation for how it had gotten on her wrist and why she couldn't get it off. Underneath the bracelet her skin was still tender from her attempts to get the bracelet off yesterday.

Then there was Jason. She wasn't sure what to think about him. On one hand she was attracted to him but on the other there was a dangerous side to him that scared her. She thought of how he had looked when he had realized what Vince had done and she shivered.

Emma shook herself free of these thoughts and refocused on driving. They had just left Chris Miller's house thirty minutes ago and were driving down a piece of road that was nicknamed The Stretch. It was a narrow forest road that wound and curved it's way down the mountain with no houses or buildings of any sort. The only light Emma had to see by came from the moon and the truck's headlights, which only illuminated the road twenty feet in front of the truck and a few feet of the forest.

There was nothing to see out there but a continuing road and a bunch of trees but Emma knew they were approaching the most infamous portion of The Stretch, Death Valley. Snake river, the largest river coming down out of the mountains, had a nasty reputation for having a vicious current that was almost impossible to survive. It had carved its way through the mountains in a deep ravine that was usually far away from every well-traveled road. Except at one point, Coffin Corner.

That wasn't the official name for the sharp corner on the Stretch that was just twenty feet from the Snake River ravine but that's what everyone at her school called it. Every few years someone took the corner too quickly and sent their car tumbling off the cliff and into the ravine. No one ever survived. Emma didn't like this area and almost never drove through it if there was any way she could avoid it. To be honest, the place creeped her out, she got goose bumps every time she drove by it.

Emma refocused her gaze inside the truck. The cab of the truck was dark. The only light was from the stereo and it cast a blue glow on Emma and Mark, creating strange shadows on their faces. She couldn't see Mark's expression, his face was turned towards the window as he stared out at the night. He had one arm wrapped around his ribs, pressing the icepack against his side and she wondered if one of his ribs had been cracked. Vince had used his whole body when he kicked Mark. It would be a miracle if he didn't.

"How are you feeling Mark?" Emma asked softly, hesitant to break the silence.

For a moment Mark said nothing, then he turned to look at her. From the stiff way he shifted it was clear he was in pain. "I'm fine." He said simply. Then he gave her a small, tight smile. "I almost had him though, a few more seconds and I would have got him."

Emma chuckled, "I know, I could see that." She frowned slightly, chewing on her lower lip for a moment before she spoke again. "I'm sorry for getting you into this." She whispered.

Mark looked over at her in confusion. "What do you mean?"

"I never should have asked you to go to that party with me. I didn't belong there and now you're hurt." Emma said.

Mark shook his head. "Emma you can't blame yourself for other people's actions. It was my choice to come and it was my choice to stand up to Vince. You aren't responsible for that."

They were silent for a moment. The headlights reflected off of a series of orange signs indicating a sharp left turn ahead. They had reached Coffin Corner. Emma began slowing down, easing back from 50 mph to less than 30.

"Do you think any of your ribs are cracked?" She asked, turning the steering wheel to take the corner.

Mark laughed and waved off her concern. "It's going to take a lot more than a little kick to the ribs to hurt me." He said confidently. "Besides I…"

Mark's next words were cut off as halfway through the corner there was a loud pop and the car jerked to the right. Emma slammed on the brakes and cranked the wheel to the left, trying to control the car but it was no use.

For a heart stopping moment she watched the truck head straight towards the steel railing along the side of the road and knew there was nothing she could do to stop it. Mark was yelling something but she couldn't hear what he was saying, her brain was frozen in shock. Just before they hit the steel railing Mark jumped across her, shielding her with his body.

Emma didn't see the impact. She only remembered a sharp jolt, then a moment of weightlessness before being tossed around. Her memory blacked out at that point. When Emma regained consciousness she was hanging upside down in the truck, her seat belt the only thing holding her in place. Blood pooled in Emma's head, putting pressure on her brain and making her thoughts fuzzy.

She saw a giant hole in the windshield, red glistened on the edges of the jagged glass. A giant tree trunk crumpled in the hood. The truck must have hit the tree when it slid down the embankment. Emma blinked, trying to clear her thoughts. She looked over to see if Mark was okay but the seat next to her was empty. Emma's thoughts began to spin and blackness rushed across her eyes, dragging her back into unconsciousness.

In the forest everything stood still. There was no movement in the woods, no sounds from the animals, the only sound was the hiss of the truck's engine as steam billowed from under the crumpled hood. Mark lay face down on the ground, unmoving. Blood was smeared across his head, matting his hair into clumps. Another moment passed.

Suddenly Mark groaned. Slowly sliding his hands up next to his shoulders he carefully rolled over, grunting in pain when the movement sent a stab of pain through his chest. Looking down Mark saw a giant shard of glass sticking out of the right side of his chest. Gripping the shard in his hands, Mark took a deep breath and yanked it out, almost passing out again from the pain.

"Ouch, that looked like it hurt."

The mocking voice came from a few feet to his left. Mark jerked around, shuffling backwards until his back was against the nearest tree, holding the shard in front of him like a weapon. Loraine leaned against a pine tree a little ways away, her arms folded across her chest and an evil smile on her face.

"You're like the poster child for why you should wear a seat belt." Loraine continued with a smirk.

"You…did you do this?" Mark ground out, clenching his teeth against the pain.

"Yes, I did." Loraine said matter-of-factly. There was no remorse in her voice or expression. She watched, unimpressed, as Mark tried to stand up.

"Emma." Mark said, looking around in a panic. "Where's Emma?"

"The human girl?" Loraine asked disinterestedly, examining her nails. "Well, I haven't heard any sound from her, so she's probably dead."

"I'm going to kill you!" Mark yelled, stumbling to his feet. He leaned against the tree, dragging raspy breaths into his lungs, but he held the glass shard in front of him threateningly. Loraine rolled her eyes.

"No, you're not." She said, her voice bored. She waved her hand and the shard flew out of Mark's hand, landing several feet away from him. Mark tried to charge at her but she laughed and flicked her hand, throwing Mark back against the tree he had been leaning against. Stunned by the impact he crumpled to the ground, panting.

"Why?" He bit out.

"Why what?" Loraine asked, examining her nails of her other hand now.

"Why did you do this?" Mark snarled.

"A few reasons really." Loraine mused, shifting her attention away from her nails to look back at him. She began sauntering towards him, in no apparent rush. "For starters I have a few questions that you have been avoiding answering. My boss is getting impatient and so am I." She stopped when she stood over him. "I figured this would be the best way to get your attention."

"And what were your other reasons?" Mark asked, glaring up at her.

"Oh, boredom and I wanted to see if you really are as pathetic as you made yourself seem back there. Letting a drunk teenage boy beat up on you? You might as well be human for how worthless you were." Loraine sneered at him. "You deserved to be punished for belittling our kind like that."

"It is no insult to me to say I am like a human. Our abilities do not make us better than them. Usually they make us worse." Mark replied.

Loraine backhanded him across the face. "You are weak and pathetic." She hissed. "Only fools believe that."

"Then I am a fool." Mark replied steadily.

"Where is Tyler?" Loraine snapped at him. Mark blinked and looked up at her in confusion.

"Tyler?" He asked. "Why do you think I would know where he is? Tyler disappeared years ago."

"After he found the journal he was making his way back to The Blade when somehow he found out that we were after him. He disappeared, taking the journals with him. We know he came here, Mark. Where is he?" Loraine stood over him, her stance uncompromising.

"I don't know." Mark told her tiredly. "He didn't come to me."

"Then where would he have gone? You are the only one with abilities in this town who has been here since before Tyler left." Loraine said.

"I don't know!" Mark snapped. "I'm not a part of your war. I'm not involved in any of this."

"You are one of us, that *makes* you involved."

Just then a noise came from the truck. Mark froze, his heightened hearing stretched to its limit.

"Mark?" Emma's voice called out weakly. "Mark? Where are you?"

"Emma!" Mark yelled back, trying to jump to his feet.

"I don't think so." Loraine hissed, holding up her hand and pinning him against the tree with an invisible force.

"Let me go!" Mark yelled at her. "Emma! I'm right here! Are you hurt?" He struggled against the invisible bonds, his face turning red.

"I-I think I'm fine." Emma stuttered. "Where are you? I can't see you. Are you okay?" Panic made Emma's voice shrill, she was trying to be calm but it wasn't working. Mark struggled again to get free.

"I'm okay Emma, just get out of the truck." Mark directed her, keeping his voice calm.

"I can't! My seatbelt is jammed. I can't get out!" Emma's voice was edging towards hysteria.

"I guess she's alive after all." Loraine commented, crossing her arms over her chest.

"Let me go." Mark growled. "I need to go make sure she's okay."

"Well obviously she's okay, she was just yelling at you." Loraine pointed out.

"LET ME GO!" Mark roared, struggling to get free with renewed effort.

"This girl really means a lot to you, doesn't she?" Loraine's voice sounded intrigued, and a little disgusted. "Letting yourself develop feelings for a human, that is a huge mistake. Humans are fragile, easily killed. She wouldn't survive for long in our world." Loraine paused, tapping a finger thoughtfully against her chin. "But you know that, don't you? That's why you're slumming it here as a barista in some nothing town. You're trying to live as a human."

Mark said nothing, he just glared at her as he struggled to get free.

"That is so…pathetic." Loraine said, shaking her head at him. "I'd be doing you a favor if I killed her right now so you could move on and live like a man with your abilities should."

"If you hurt her I swear I will spend the rest of my life making yours a living hell!" Mark threatened.

Loraine stared at him, her gaze ice cold. "Tell me what you know and I'll let the girl live."

"I don't know anything. How many times do I have to tell you that?" Mark snapped.

"That doesn't do me any good, now does it?" Loraine snarled back. Then she paused and a sadistic smile touched her face. "But I'm a bit of a romantic so I'll let her live."

Mark stopped struggling for a moment, locking his gaze with hers. "You will?" He said, his voice suspicious.

Loraine nodded, smiling generously. "Of course I will!" She said cheerfully. "As long as you can get to her in time." With a flick of her wrist the truck was pushed off the tree it was propped against and sent tumbling towards the ravine again.

"NOOOO!!!" Mark yelled as Emma screamed, surging to his feet and racing after the truck. Mark caught up to the truck and grabbed the front end, managing to keep it upright but he was too weak to stop it. The truck continued to slide backwards towards the ravine. Realizing he couldn't hold it Mark jumped on top of the hood and scrambled towards Emma who was frantically clawing at her seatbelt.

"Mark!" She yelled, feeling a surge of relief when she saw him. "Help! It's stuck!"

Tree branches snapped as the truck crashed by and the uneven ground jolted Emma and Mark as the truck bounced along, faster and faster down the hill. The ravine was only 20 yards away and the truck was gaining momentum. Emma felt her heart race as panic rushed through her.

Mark was clinging to the hood of the truck, blood seeping through his shirt. She had no idea how he was hanging on but she had never seen him look so determined. Tears pricked at her eyes. This was how she was going to die, falling into Death Valley like so many others. Mark reached into the cab of the truck through the hole in the windshield and grabbed her seatbelt.

"It's stuck!" Emma tried to tell him but before the words had finished leaving her mouth there was the sound of groaning metal and the seatbelt snapped.

"Crawl out!" Mark yelled.

The truck bounced and Emma had to quickly grab the steering wheel to keep from hitting the roof of the cab. Mark gestured more urgently. The ravine was getting closer. Tucking her legs up underneath her on the seat Emma crawled onto the dashboard and through the hole in the windshield. When she was partly through Mark wrapped an arm around her waist and hoisted her out just as the back of the truck fell off the cliff.

Planting his feet beneath him Mark jumped back towards the edge of the cliff where a thick tree root protruded from the cliff face, Emma firmly wrapped in his arms. The truck disappeared beneath them. For a moment in time they were held suspended in thin air as Mark made a desperate reach for the root, but his grasping fingers were feet away from being able to grab their only lifeline. As they plummeted into a free fall their momentum carried them towards the cliff face. Mark curled his body protectively around Emma's, tucking her against his chest.

Mark watched the cliff face come closer. They were going to hit it before they ever reach the river. Mark tucked his legs up, buying them some time. There, Mark saw a boulder in the cliff face that was a smooth surface. As they were just about to hit it Mark slammed his legs out, pushing off of the rock and propelling him and Emma out over the river.

Below them he could see the rocks jutting up out of the rushing water. It would be a miracle if they didn't hit them. They probably wouldn't survive, but Mark had given Emma the best chance he could. Mark closed his eyes and held Emma close, waiting for the impact.

Emma surfaced from the river with a gasp. Waves slapped her face, splashing water into her mouth and choking her. She sputtered, gasping in as much air as she could without inhaling water as well. Panic choked at her throat.

The last thing she remembered was Mark jumping back towards the cliff. After that was blackness. A big wave submerged her and Emma fought to pull her head above water again. Her clothes and shoes were heavy with water, they were dragging her down towards the bottom of the river. She could feel herself being rushed along with the current. Who knew how far she was down river now.

In between waves Emma got a glance of the riverbank and furiously began to swim towards it. The rivers current was so strong that she was a good quarter of a mile downstream by the time she reached the shore.

Emma collapsed onto the ground, panting from exertion. The night air was cold, the wind mercilessly sliced through her clothes to her wet skin. Within seconds she was shivering. For a few moments she just lay there, unable to move. She was so tired, she didn't think she had any strength left in her.

Then like a bolt of lightning the memory of Mark pulling her from the truck and holding her as they fell hit her. Adrenaline pounded through her system, wiring her with energy. Emma scrambled to her feet, frantically searching for Mark.

"Mark!" She screamed. "Mark!"

No yells answered her panicked scream. Tears pricked at her eyes. She didn't know where to look for him first or if he had even survived their fall. Emma angrily banished that thought from her mind. Of course he had survived, he *had* to.

Torn between searching up or down the river she hesitated on the bank for a moment, looking back and forth. Finally she decided to find the truck and search downriver from there. Emma took off running, scrambling over rocks and past bushes as she tried to find where they had fallen. It turned out finding it wasn't difficult. Mark's truck stuck straight up in the river, the force of the fall lodging it firmly in the riverbed. The headlights were like twin beams that shot straight into the air, illuminating the area around the car.

"Mark!" Emma called out, hoping he was nearby.

Emma didn't see any sign of him or hear a response. It was difficult to see in the dark, even with the headlights of the truck still on. Emma was just about to move on downstream when she caught sight of a large tree branch that was half in and half out of the water on the other side of the river.

102

A large boulder just upriver sheltered the area from the harsh current and the bank curved to accommodate a small pool of circling water that was sheltered from the harsh current, which was why the branch hadn't been washed downstream. She didn't know what had caught her eye but when she looked back she saw a flash of brown hair floating near the branch.

"Mark!" Emma yelled, diving back into the water. She struggled against the current, fighting to get to the branch. Reaching shore a few feet away from the tree branch she dragged herself out of the water and ran over to it. Mark was there, floating face down in the river. One of his arms had gotten wedged in one of the branches, which was why the river hadn't dragged him downstream too.

Emma jumped in the water and grabbed him under the arms, dragging him out of the river and onto the bank. He was a lot heavier than she realized. She only managed to drag half of his body out of the river before she fell back in the dirt, exhausted.

Scrambling to her feet she immediately checked for his pulse. Her fingers were so cold that at first she couldn't feel anything because they were shaking so hard but after blowing on them a few times to warm them up she finally felt his pulse. She sighed in relief when she felt it beating strongly and sagged against him.

"Mark, can you hear me? Please wake up!" Emma said, shaking him by the shoulders. She knew that wasn't the proper way to handle things but she was too freaked out to do anything else.

Mark jolted upright, gasping for breath, then rolled over as he started coughing up river water.

"Oh thank god you're alright!" Emma said, throwing herself on him and giving him a hug.

"Ribs." Mark gasped, wincing in pain.

"Sorry!" Emma apologized, immediately letting go. "I'm just so glad you're alive! When I saw you floating there I thought you were dead!"

"Not that easy. To kill. Me." Mark grunted, wincing in pain. He wrapped an arm around his ribs and fell back on the riverbank.

"We need to get you to the hospital." Emma said. "My phone's in the truck." She looked over at the truck, noticing how it was half filled with water. "So the water has probably ruined it." She groaned.

Mark grabbed her arm to get her attention, half sitting up so he could see her more clearly. "Are you okay?" He asked. His eyes were cloudy from pain but he still focused on her, checking her for any injuries.

Emma paused, considering his question. "Yeah." She replied in shock. "I'm fine."

"Fine?" Mark asked as if he couldn't believe it either.

"I don't think I'm hurt." Emma said, looking at her arms and legs as if expecting to find blood or something. "How is that even possible?"

Mark shook his head. "Don't know." He grunted, giving up on sitting up and falling onto his back again. He groaned when he hit the ground, his face twisting in pain.

Emma looked at him lying on the bank. He had several cuts on his hands and arms and she could already see some bruising on his face. "We really need to get you help. Can you move?"

"I need to rest a while." Mark mumbled. His wet hair clung to his head and Emma winced when she saw that the water trickling out of his hair was tinged pink with his blood. "I should be able to move soon."

"I'm going to try to find my phone and a first aid kit in the truck. I'll be right back." Emma promised. Her phone was probably ruined but there was a slight chance it wasn't and she would try anything right then.

She waded back into the water and swam to the truck, climbing inside through one of the broken windows. She managed to find a first aid kit floating around near the back seats and her purse was still in the front of the truck. Grabbing both she did her best to hold them out of the water as she swam back to Mark.

Dumping her purse upside down on the riverbank she snatched her phone up, letting out a cheer when it still worked. The heavy-duty protective case Mark had given her when she got her phone because of how accident prone she was had protected the phone from water damage. Emma called 9-1-1 as she ripped open the first aid kit and started cleaning Mark's wounds as best as she could. She told the operator what had happened and where they were, hanging up when the operator told her that someone was on the way.

Emma wrapped Mark in the thermal blanket she had found and settled his head in her lap, stroking his hair.

"We're going to be okay Mark." She whispered. "We're going to be okay."

The doctors said it was a miracle that Emma and Mark survived the crash. The fact that Emma walked away without a scratch was impossible. They wanted to examine her more, figure out how she had escaped such a terrible crash without an injury but Steve absolutely forbade it.

After making her stay under observation for 24 hours Emma was released, but not before Steve had made each of the doctors who had heard the story sign a confidentiality agreement. Neither Steve nor Mark wanted to have the story on the news. Steve said that because of the traumatic nature of the accident he thought it would be better if no one found out about it so that Emma could move on without being constantly reminded of what had happened. Mark had agreed. No one had asked Emma.

Mark had to stay in the hospital for a few days. His injuries weren't severe, again much to the doctor's shock, but he did have a cracked rib and his body had gone through extreme shock so the doctor thought it would be best to keep him under observation. Mark wasn't happy about the situation but he was still too weak to argue with the doctor about it.

Before Emma left the hospital she stopped into Mark's room to see him.

"Hey." She murmured, walking over to the side of his hospital bed.

Wires dangled from his bed and connected to monitors. Mark's head was wrapped in a bandage and his ribs had been stabilized. The doctors told her he was recovering very well. They expected him to make a full recovery in no time.

"Hey." Mark's voice was gravelly. He tried to push himself up in the bed but winced and fell back.

"Careful, your ribs are going to need a lot of time to heal. You may want to take it easy on them." Emma cautioned him. She sat down in the chair angled next to his bed while Mark carefully eased himself into a sitting position.

"Yeah, that's what the doctor's have been telling me. I keep hoping they are wrong though." Mark replied with a grimace. "So are you getting out of here today?" He looked at Emma's outfit and the purse she held clutched in her hand.

"Yep, Kathryn is waiting for me in the lobby. I just wanted to come check on you before I left." Emma told him.

Mark nodded. "I'm glad you're okay."

Emma was quiet for a moment. Then she looked up at Mark's battered face and her eyebrows slanted downwards as she struggled to phrase a question that had been bugging her all day.

"Mark?"

"Yes, Em?"

"Do you remember what happened that night?"

Mark was silent. He stared down at his hands and then looked at her. Emma began talking again, filling the awkward silence. "I just don't remember much. There was the crash, then the truck hit a tree. I could have sworn I heard you talking to someone out there. Then the car started rolling again and once we fell off the cliff...nothing. It's just black for me."

Mark shook his head slowly. "I wasn't talking to anyone." He told her. "Once I got thrown out of the truck I was knocked unconscious. I only woke up just in time to see the truck start rolling again. I ran after it to try to pull you out, and I tried to jump back onto the cliff but I was too late. I vaguely remember falling and wishing I could have saved you. Then that's it."

Emma nodded silently, staring down at her hands as she thought of what he had said. Guilt for not telling her she was the reason they had survived plucked at him but he pushed it aside. He didn't know what had happened or how she had done what she did. When he figured it out then he would tell her.

"Okay, well I should be going. Kathryn is waiting for me." Emma stood up and smiled down at Mark.

"I don't know how we survived, but I'm glad we did." She said, patting him on the arm.

Mark nodded and gave her a slight wave as she walked out, a troubled expression on his face.

106

The accident didn't keep Kathryn and Steve from grounding Emma once they found out she had gotten another detention. Aside from school and work Emma wasn't allowed to go anywhere or hang out with anyone. With Mark in the hospital Emma didn't have any reason to go to the coffee shop after school anyways. Besides, the one thing she was really interested was at home.

Once she had gotten over the shock of the accident Emma had refocused on the mystery bracelet. Or more accurately, how to get it off of her. She had found the bracelet in the box of things she had found so maybe there was something in there that could explain what it was. The most likely source of information seemed to be the diary she had found so Emma spent the week pouring through the diary, trying to find any mention of the bracelet.

Before she could find anything about the bracelet she stumbled across something even more confusing.

March 22, 1990
Dear Diary,
The things I can do now scare me. I don't want this ability. I can't even tell my brothers what is happening. If they knew that I am a Secret Stealer they would never speak to me again. But I am so scared of what I'm turning into. The stories I've heard of Secret Stealers, none of them are good. They are terrible people, and most of them end up going crazy. I don't want that to be me but I can't change what I am.

So far there has only been one good thing about being a Secret Stealer. Today I met Ryker Forgeron, a boy just two years older than me. He is so lost and confused, he doesn't even know what's real anymore. He was standing on the cliffs about to jump when he saw me walking by the river. I was so lost in my own thoughts I didn't notice that there was a man following me. I didn't even realize I was about to be attacked until it was too late. The man pulled a knife on me and then out of nowhere Ryker appeared and fought him off.

Afterwards when we talked I discovered what he had been about to do. I told him I could help, and for the first time I saw a glimmer of hope in his eyes. We make an interesting pair. The boy who can change reality and the girl who always sees the truth. And yet, he understands me better than anyone else.

When Emma read that entry she had set the journal down on her desk and leaned back in her chair. Ryker Forgeron? Emma walked over to the closet and dug the picture out of the box. What if this couple was Ryker and Alexandra? They had fallen in love and had a daughter. Emma smiled wistfully. It was a romantic story, two people save each other and fall in love. It didn't tell her anything about the bracelet but it was still a good story.

It wasn't until two days later that Emma finally stumbled across a passage mentioning the bracelet. She was reclining in her bed, pillows propped up behind her back and she read through Alexandra's journal and snacked on a bowl of chocolate covered pretzels. As soon as she stumbled across the entry she set the bowl on the bedside table, focusing completely on what Alexandra had said.

October 7, 1991
The fights between my brothers are getting worse. I don't know how much longer I can handle this. I want to get away from them, to escape from all their anger and this life that I am trapped in. Ryker is worried about me. I know my brothers would never hurt me but he isn't so sure. Today he gave me a bracelet, it has three strands of leather with flat metal disks woven into the design. Ryker told me to always wear it, that the bracelet would protect me even when he couldn't. I thought it was just a good luck charm but he made me promise to never take it off so maybe there is more to this bracelet than I know.

That was all that Alexandra said about the bracelet. Emma skimmed through the next few entries to see if she mentioned it again but she didn't.

Leaning back against the headrest of her bed Emma sighed and looked up at the ceiling of her room. A bracelet that mysteriously attaches itself to her and refuses to let go, Ryker making Alexandra promise never to take it off, what was it about this bracelet that was so special? And Emma wasn't any closer to figuring out how to get the stupid thing off of her.

If Ryker believed the bracelet would protect its wearer somehow, was it just a coincidence she was wearing the same bracelet that's supposed to protect her right before she walked away from an accident that should have killed her?

Emma felt like she had just found more questions instead of answers.

CHAPTER EIGHT

A few weeks passed by uneventfully. Emma would go to school in the morning, then after school she would stop by the coffee shop to say hi to Mark and get her coffee before heading over to the bookstore to work. Emma liked working at the bookstore, it was quiet and Mrs. White didn't mind if she did her homework there as long as there was nothing she needed to do, which there almost never was.

Most days Emma didn't get home until ten, which was when her parents would tell Jason he needed to leave. Jason and Morgan were hanging out almost every day now, something Emma was less than thrilled about but as long as she wasn't there to see it she didn't have too much of a problem with it.

Emma had other things she was more worried about. Ever since the accident her headaches had become more frequent. Any time her emotions were raised would bring on a stab of pain, and instead of becoming less emotional her emotions were becoming heightened. The littlest thing would set her off and then she would get a headache and have to calm herself down.

She discovered that going for long runs helped a lot so every morning Emma continued to wake up early and go for long runs to help her keep it together throughout the day. For the most part she succeeded in convincing everyone that everything was normal and she was fine. Of course Mark wasn't so easily fooled.

"It's getting worse, isn't it?" He asked, coming and sitting in the chair next to hers.

It was Sunday afternoon. Emma had the day off and only two or three other people were in the coffee shop. It was her favorite time to hang out there. The smell of the coffee and the sound of the music playing over the speakers always relaxed her. It was also the one time when Mark could sit with her for more than a few seconds.

Emma hadn't even noticed she was rubbing her forehead again until Mark said something. It was such an unconscious gesture by this point that she rarely noticed herself doing it. The buzzing in her head was worse today and her head still ached from the huge fight she and Morgan had gotten into before Emma left.

It had started over such a stupid little thing too. Morgan had taken too long of a shower and had used up all the hot water so that Emma had to take a cold one that morning. So Emma had snapped at Morgan, who had snapped right back, and pretty soon the entire argument had escalated until the two were screaming at each other and Kathryn had to separate them. Which was the other reason why Emma was sitting in the coffee shop that afternoon.

Emma dropped her hand into her lap. "What's getting worse?" She asked innocently.

"The headaches. I can tell they have been so don't try to hide it." Mark said, his voice serious. His deep brown eyes looked at her with concern and a slight bit of annoyance. He hated when she lied to him.

"I'm fine, don't worry about it." Emma tried to brush it off, even though she knew that would just make him fixate on it more.

"No, you're not fine." Mark insisted. Emma sighed and rolled her eyes. He was going to start lecturing her. "Ever since the accident your headaches have been getting worse, you are losing weight despite the fact that you are eating five times more food than you usually do and your emotions are out of control."

Emma looked down at her clothes. She hadn't really thought about it but they were getting a little big on her. She plucked at the waistline of her pants held up by a belt that was so loose it was hardly worth wearing. She should probably go shopping pretty soon.

"Emma?" Mark's voice cut into her thoughts.

"What?" She asked, her voice a little sharper than she intended.

Mark blew out a breath, looking slightly frustrated. "I want you to talk to me!" He snapped.

"There isn't anything to talk about!" Emma snapped back, feeling the familiar sharp pang in her head. "Yes, my headaches are getting worse, and yes my emotions are out of control but I don't know what you want me to do about that!"

"Maybe you should go see a doctor or something." Mark suggested, softening his voice.

Emma immediately felt bad for snapping at him. He was just worried about her and she thanked him by biting his head off. What a great friend she was turning out to be.

"I don't need to see a doctor." Emma said mulishly.

"You need to do something." Mark said, his voice concerned. "This isn't healthy."

Emma shrugged. "I'll be fine." She said.

A customer walked in and stood at the counter waiting to order. Mark gave her a long look before sighing and walking off. Emma stared out the window at the beautiful day outside without seeing anything. Mark was right, there was something wrong with her. She just didn't know what.

The next day Emma was at work later than usual. Mrs. White had left as soon as Emma got there and had given Emma a long list of tasks that needed to be completed that night. Normally it wouldn't have been much of a problem but her headaches had been so bad that day that it was taking her much longer than it should have to get everything done. It was almost eleven when Emma finally locked up and started walking to her car.

Her car was parked a couple of stores down because of how full the parking lot had been that afternoon so she walked along the sidewalk in front of the stores, hurrying a little bit in the cold night air. All the other stores had long since been closed, the owners had gone home to be with their families. Emma saw a light on in the coffee shop even though it had closed a few hours ago. Someone must be doing inventory or something like that. She hoped it wasn't Mark who was stuck working late.

The night was darker than usual. There was no moon out to see by and the few stars that could be seen were obscured by stray clouds. The only source of light was the evenly spaced lampposts along the street on the other side of the dark parking lot. A light breeze blew through the parking lot, catching dry leaves and skittering them across the pavement.

Emma tugged her coat tighter around her and shrugged her shoulders up around her ears. The haunting sound of a wind chime drifted on the breeze and somewhere a loose windowpane clacked against a building. Emma's senses stretched to their limit, alert for any noise or movement out of the ordinary as her feeling of unease grew.

Each of the stores had a narrow alley between them that led to a back access road behind the stores. On a night like tonight those alleys turned to dark holes of nothingness where anything could be lurking. It was impossible to see more than a few feet into the alleys because of the impenetrable blackness. Emma had no idea what might be lurking in the darkness as she passed by one of the alleys but her overactive imagination was throwing out plenty of ideas.

Emma was just passing the alleyway between the coffee shop and the old antique shop next to it when she thought she heard something strange coming from the darkness. She froze, ears straining to hear what it might have been. The noise came again, a scuffle followed by a thud and a groan of pain. The murmur of voices drifted down the alley but she couldn't hear what they were saying.

Emma glanced over at her car just thirty feet away. The safest, and probably smartest, thing to do would be to run to her car and drive away as fast as possible. Emma heard another groan of pain and before she realized what she was doing she was creeping down the alley, following some mysterious impulse.

Luckily the shopping district Emma worked in was a nice one, the alleyways between stores were kept clean and clear so she didn't have to worry about giving away her presence by running into anything in the darkness. The further she crept into the alley the darker the inky blackness grew until she could hardly see anything in front of her, even after her eyes adjusted to the darkness.

Emma's pulse pounded in her ears, her adrenaline causing her heart to race in fear or anticipation, she didn't know which. The soft-soled shoes she was wearing hardly made any noise as she walked back through the alley and Emma had the random thought that she was glad she hadn't worn the high heels she had planned on wearing that day.

Emma could see light glowing from the road behind the stores as she gradually made her way closer. Each store had a light above its back door so the owners could see what they were doing when they took the trash out to the dumpsters behind their shops. When Emma reached the end of the alley she crouched just inside of the entrance, carefully scanning the area around her.

Off to the left she heard the murmur of men's voices but her view was blocked by a dumpster. Emma hesitated, torn between the urge to find out what was happening and the urge to get out of there as quickly as possible. In the end her curiosity won out and she crept forward, using the dumpster to hide behind as she peered around it.

Three men stood in a loose semi circle around a crumpled body. One of them was an absolute giant, Emma had never seen anyone so big in her life. He had a wicked looking scar from just above his right eye all the way down his face and through the right side of his mouth. The scar distorted his lips, making him seem like he was always snarling. He had long shaggy blonde hair that was a combination of dreadlocks and thick braids. He resembled what Emma imagined a cave man must have looked like. The giant motioned at the body, whispering something to the man next to him who was the obvious leader. That was when Emma noticed his hands. Bigger than they should have been even for a man of his size, what caught Emma's attention were the claws that were on the end of his fingers where fingernails should have been. Black as night and wickedly sharp, they could easily tear someone to shreds. When the giant spoke Emma saw a flash of fangs and barely choked back a whimper. Whatever that man was, he wasn't human.

Emma looked at the man closest to her. He was small and slender, petite next to the giant. His hair was jet black and slicked back out of his face. There was no hint of emotion on his face, his expression was cold and distant. In his hands he held two knives that he whirled around and around, so fast they were a blur but the man showed no sign of exerting himself. Suddenly the daggers

114

stopped whirling and before Emma could blink they were gone. She hadn't even seen him move his hands to sheath them, they were just in his hands one moment and gone the next.

In between the giant and the knife fighter stood a third man who was the obvious leader of the group. He was dressed impeccably in a dark grey suit, his light brown hair perfectly cut and styled, his hands encased in expensive looking black leather gloves. The man looked like he should be in a Fortune 500 company boardroom instead of in a back alley of a small town-shopping district. There was something about the man that gave Emma the creeps though. His eyes were black pits in his face, no hint of emotion touched them, just cold ruthlessness. With a jolt Emma realized that she recognized him. He was the man from the nightmare she had a few weeks ago.

"This is getting us nowhere, Greco." The knife fighter hissed.

The man in the suit, Greco, nodded at the giant next to him who leaned down and grabbed the body on the ground, easily lifting it into the air. A groan came from the body, whoever it was he was still alive.

"Tell me where the journal is." Greco commanded. His voice gave Emma the chills. It was so cold and empty of emotion. This man would have no problem killing anyone who got in his way.

When the man didn't respond the giant shook him roughly. He made a noise, somewhere between a laugh and a hacking cough. When he lifted his head Emma got a clear look at his face. It was the man from the coffee shop!

Emma bit back a gasp, tears pricking at her eyes. Tyler's curly brown hair was matted with filth, or blood, and his square jaw was mottled with bruises.

"You're never going to find it." Tyler said, his voice hoarse and tired. "Kill me if you want but there is no way I'm telling you where it is."

"Oh, I'm not going to kill you." Greco said calmly, slowly taking off his gloves. "There's a reason I am sent when someone needs to be persuaded to talk." He nodded at the giant again who ripped the front of the Tyler's shirt open, leaving his chest bare to the cold night air.

"Do you know what it feels like to have every nerve ending in your body screaming in pain?" He asked softly, removing his coat and carefully folding it before handing it to the knife wielder along with his gloves. "All it takes is one touch of my hand and you'll find out for yourself. I've heard it feels like being burned from the inside out. Don't worry, no physical damage is actually done so you won't die. At least not until I want you to." He said.

Greco slowly began rolling up the sleeves of his expensive shirt, continuing to talk.

"Some people have gone mad from the pain, but I'm not too worried about that. Mad people can still talk after all, and sometimes they say more than those who are sane. Of course, you could skip all of that pain if you told me where the journal was. Ethan could just snap your neck and it would all be over, a quick and painless death."

Tyler just shook his head tiredly. "Go to hell."

"You should have gone with the quick death." Greco replied coldly, placing his hand on Tyler's chest. The skin where his hand touched turned a bright red and Tyler screamed, the sound so full of pain it was unearthly. His face contorted in agony and the screaming went on and on as he thrashed about. Ethan gripped Tyler more securely, restraining his movements as the torture continued.

Tears streamed down Emma's face at the sound of it, she had never heard anything so horrible in her entire life. Greco lifted his hand from Tyler's chest and Tyler's head dropped in exhaustion.

"Do you feel like telling me where the journal is now, Tyler?" He asked, his voice calm as if he hadn't just caused another human so much pain.

"Never." Tyler rasped. His voice shredded from his screaming. He didn't even have the strength to hold his own head up anymore. Emma couldn't handle seeing someone in so much pain, she had to help him.

"Obviously I haven't convinced you enough, let's try this again." Greco said, reaching his hand forward.

"Stop!" Emma yelled, leaping out from her hiding place. "You're killing him!"

The men all stared at her in surprise, caught off guard by her appearance. Emma was a little surprised by her sudden appearance as well. Tyler lifted his head to see who had stopped his tormentors. When he saw her the blood drained out of his face like he had seen a ghost.

"Alexandra?" He rasped. When the other three men got over their surprise they looked at each other, clearly recognizing the name. They shifted in her direction, clearly intending on going after her. Tyler's expression changed to panic.

"Run!" He yelled. "You know where the journal is, don't let them get it!"

"Get her!" Greco snapped at the knife wielder. Tyler continued yelling at Emma to run, thrashing around in Ethan's grip. "Ethan shut him up!"

The giant hit Tyler on the side of the head, knocking him out and cutting off Tyler's yell in mid scream.

Emma watched everything like it was happening in slow motion. Tyler's body falling to the floor, the small man sprinting towards her as a knife reappeared in his hand. A small voice somewhere in Emma's head yelled at her to run away but it was lost under the wave of panic that filled Emma at the sight of Tyler lying on the ground, his shirt torn and blood and dirt smeared on his face. Emma was frozen, her fear paralyzing her. She just kept looking at Tyler's body, unable to process what had just happened.

She saw the small man running towards her, a knife in his hands and a look of deadly intent on his face. She knew she should run but she couldn't move. She just watched as he came closer. As he ran the man threw a knife at her, aiming at her leg to cripple her from running.

Emma flinched, waiting for the impact, to feel the pain of the knife slicing into her leg but nothing happened. She looked down at herself in disbelief but there was no dagger to be seen. Looking up she saw the small man stumble, covering his leg with his hand. Between his fingers lodged into his leg was the dagger that he had thrown at her. Gripping the dagger the man pulled it out of his leg in one quick movement. Blood poured from the wound, leaving a dark stain that spread down his leg.

Emma thought she was going to be sick but the man didn't seem to notice his injury. He ran towards her again, this time when he got near he launched himself at her, trying to tackle Emma to the ground. Just like the dagger though he was caught in midair and thrown backwards before he could touch her. He slammed into the wall of the coffee shop and dropped to the ground unconscious.

The sound of footsteps pounding towards her caught Emma's attention and she looked back to see the giant Ethan sprinting towards her. His face was twisted into a snarl and the claws on his hands curled as he reached them towards her, as if he wanted to rip her to shreds. In that moment Emma knew she was going to die.

"Emma!"

Emma jerked around at the sound of her name but she didn't see anything. A rush of air reminded her of Ethan's charge and she whipped back around instinctively throwing her hands up to guard her face. Ethan slammed straight into the same shield the knife wielder had hit and was flung backwards from the impact. Emma heard a sound behind her again and she turned, ready for another attack. Emma barely registered Mark's face looming above hers before the world went black.

When Emma woke up she was in her bed back home with the worst headache she had ever had. But as she lay buried under her fluffy comforter and blankets with her head cushioned on a nice soft pillow she realized that the headache she had was a normal headache. The kind of headache anyone would get if they hit their head. The thought made her grin. But then the events from the night before came pouring into her head and she jolted upright in bed with a gasp.

"Emma, calm down. You're okay." Mark sat down on the bed beside her, trying to restrain her from jumping out of bed.

"Last night, those men, they were torturing him! And me, they went after me. I just stood there, but they couldn't touch me." Emma was babbling, she knew she was, but the shock of last nights events kept the words bubbling out of her mouth. "Then you were there, and everything went black!" She exclaimed.

118

She stared at him and frowned, suddenly realizing what that meant. She jerked out of his grasp and scooted as far away from him on the bed as she could. "Why were you there last night?" She asked accusingly, hysteria edging into her voice. "And what happened to those men?"

"Emma, you need to calm down." Mark said soothingly, reaching over to pull her back towards him.

"Don't tell me I need to calm down!" Emma yelled at him, pushing his hands away. "I saw a man get tortured last night and the last thing I remember is you running at me, so don't tell me to calm down! What were you doing there?"

Mark held his hands up placatingly and leaned back to give her some space. "I was working at the coffee shop late last night. I heard the yelling and I came out to see what was happening. When I saw the men attack you I ran over to help." Mark frowned a little bit in confusion. "I don't know what had happened but one of them was already injured and the other one was just getting up again. When you turned to face me he hit you on the back of the head. That's why you blacked out. They ran off when I showed up though."

"They ran off? Just like that?" Emma said, clearly not believing him.

"Yeah, the big guy grabbed the little guy and Tyler and ran off after the man in the suit." Mark said.

"Greco." Emma said absently. She plucked at the edge of her comforter, not sure what to think of Mark's story.

"Excuse me?" Mark said, looking at her carefully. He leaned closer, planting a hand on the bed. Emma stared at his hand, wondering if she had said too much. Slowly she looked up at his face.

"The man in the suit. His name is Greco." Emma said hesitantly.

"How do you know that?" Mark asked, shifting to face her more.

Emma looked down in embarrassment "I don't want to tell you." She mumbled.

"Why not?" Mark pressed.

"Because you're going to think I'm crazy." She muttered, tugging nervously at her comforter.

"No, I won't." Mark said. He reached over to place his hand over hers on the comforter. "I would never think that." When Emma still looked torn Mark gently took her hand in his and made her look at him. "You can tell me, Em."

Emma smiled at the mention of the childhood nickname he had given her. She sighed and finally caved. "I had a dream about him and when I saw them that night one of his henchmen called him Greco."

"A dream?" Mark asked. He wasn't laughing though, so Emma continued.

"It was more of a nightmare than a dream." She explained. "In my dream I saw a huge manor in the middle of a forest. Inside the manor was a room, a study or a library I think. There was a fireplace there and a huge wing backed chair in front of it. A man was sitting in the chair but I never saw his face because the chair was always hidden in shadows." Mark's face looked serious but he was listening intently to everything that Emma was saying.

Emma had a bad feeling that he knew who the man was. "Greco walked into study. He started talking about a journal and Tyler White. He started to say something about what happened to a girl but then it was like the shadows came alive and started choking him. The man in the chair told him never to talk about her. Then they started talking about descendants and that there might be a list of them in the back of the journal." Mark was staring off into space, deep in thought. Emma pulled her hand out of his and wrapped her arms around herself. "I don't know what any of it means but when I woke up I was terrified."

"Are you sure they said Tyler White?" Mark asked her suddenly, refocusing on her.

Emma blinked, confused by the question and wondering why he was taking her dream seriously. "Yeah, it was Tyler White." She affirmed. Emma paused as she remembered something else. "The guy they were torturing last night was the guy we talked to in the coffee shop that day. He was babbling about a bunch of crazy stuff then. Do you think it could all be related?"

"I don't know." Mark said, but something in his voice made Emma think he knew more than what he was telling her.

"Mark, do you know who those men were? Do you know why they couldn't hurt me?" Emma asked, grabbing his arm.

Mark's expression was conflicted, he opened his mouth but didn't say anything. The door opened then and Kathryn came into the room. "Emma dear, you're awake!" She exclaimed, coming over to the bed and enveloping Emma in a hug. "We were so worried. I could hardly believe it when Mark told us that you had witnessed a mugging and had been hurt when you tried to help the poor man. What were you thinking? You could have been killed!"

"I'm not so sure about that anymore." Emma muttered, glaring at Mark.

Mark stood up. "I should be going, I just wanted to make sure Emma was okay," he told Kathryn.

Kathryn stood up as well, beaming at Mark. "Of course, and thank you so much for taking care of Emma like you did. You are a great friend." She gave Mark a big hug and Emma grinned at how uncomfortable Mark looked.

"Uh, of course Mrs. Wellworth." Mark muttered, his cheeks turning red from embarrassment. "I'll come back later, Em." He said, before walking out the door.

When he was gone Kathryn turned and looked at Emma, propping her hands on her hips. "That is twice in the last two months that you have almost gotten killed!" She exclaimed. "Do you intend on making this a monthly occurrence?"

Emma slouched down in her bed, trying to burrow beneath her comforter. "No." She mumbled.

"Good, I hope not." Kathryn replied. "Now that you're awake I'm going to call the doctor and have him make a house run. I don't want to take you to the hospital again if we don't have to." She said briskly.

Emma groaned. "I don't need a doctor." She grumbled. "I'm fine!"

"You suffered a blow to the head and were unconscious for twelve hours. You aren't fine." Kathryn replied tartly, pursing her lips at Emma. "Now try to rest, the doctor will be here soon." Kathryn left the room and shut the door firmly behind her.

Emma humphed and crossed her arms. Then a slow grin stretched across her face, she must have really scared Kathryn for her to shut the door so hard. Emma's mouth stretched into a huge yawn as she settled back into her bed. She was really tired. Before she fell asleep though a thought crossed her mind. If the men attacking her hadn't been able to touch her how did she get hit in the head?

Emma was having another nightmare. She was in the same room, with the same shadow covered chair in front of her. Emma looked at the black space around the chair. Slowly the shadows began to disperse. Emma was just beginning to see the outline of a man's legs when she heard someone say her name.

"Emma."

The shadows slammed down around the chair.

"You're in here, aren't you?" The voice whispered.

Shadows slid from the corners and grasped at her ankles. Emma screamed and tried to kick loose but the shadows wouldn't release their hold.

"Emma!" The voice came again, more urgently this time.

The shadows slid up her legs, grasping tighter and tighter. Emma felt her shoulders being shaken. She screamed, fighting the shadows that were pinning her legs in place, struggling to get free.

"Emma!"

With a gasp Emma jolted awake, glancing wildly around the room. Mark was bent over her, shaking her shoulders, concern written all over his face.

"Another nightmare?" Mark asked gently. He sat back down in the chair next to her bed, watching her carefully. Emma nodded absently, looking around for her clock.

"It's 4:30 in the afternoon." Mark told her. "Kathryn told me you've been sleeping all day."

Emma stared at him blankly for a moment. She heard what he said but she was having a hard time registering it. Her mind was still caught between the dream and reality. Slowly reality sank back in though and she relaxed back onto her pillows.

"I had another dream about the manor." Emma whispered. She stared blankly out of her bedroom window at the bright sunny afternoon. It was the kind of day meant for being outside with friends, laying out by a pool or floating down the river. Out the window off in the distance she heard children shrieking with laughter and calling out to each other, their voices young and bright.

Mark watched her closely. Emma was pale and she kept chewing at her lip with her teeth. Her hands were shaking as she smoothed them over the comforter.

"Let's go for a walk." Mark said brightly, standing up. "You've been inside all day. I think a little sunshine will be good for you."

Emma continued to stare blankly out of the window. She showed no sign that she had heard Mark. Then she slowly dragged her gaze away from the window to look at him. The dreams still weighed heavy on her mind but she could see Mark was trying hard to cheer her up so she nodded her head. "Okay." She agreed quietly. "A little sunshine might be a good thing."

Mark smiled in relief and left to tell Kathryn. Once Emma had changed and was ready to go, Mark led her outside to the backyard. Emma took a deep breath of the sweet spring air, allowing the sunshine and fresh air to relax her and bring her back to reality. The sun was shining and the birds were singing. It was a beautiful spring day, and it reminded her that this was what was real, not the dark manor in her nightmares.

"You want to tell me about your dream?" Mark asked. He walked slowly next to her, matching his pace to Emma's slow meandering stride. His hands were tucked into the pockets of his jeans, and he chewed absently on a blade of grass but Emma could sense his tension. Emma stared off in the distance as she thought of how to describe it.

"It was the same as the last one, the manor, the study, the man sitting in a chair covered by shadows. Greco walked in. The Shadow Man seemed unhappy that he had returned without the journal but Greco told him there was something he would want to know." Here Emma paused, taking a deep breath to fortify her nerves. Mark reached out and took one of her hands in his. The feel of his warm, rough hand against her own was comforting.

Drawing strength from the contact Emma continued to tell Mark about the dream. "Greco started telling the Shadow Man about what happened last night, about me. He said I was using a shield to block the attacks last night and when he mentioned that Tyler had called me Alexandra the Shadow Man told Greco to bring me to him. Greco said they would have last night if…" Emma stopped talking again.

Mark squeezed her hand reassuringly. "If what, Em?"

"If you hadn't shown up." Emma told him. She watched him carefully to see how he would react to what she was going to say next. "He said you were the one who knocked me out and that you fought Ethan. But that's not what you said. You said they ran off when you showed up and that Ethan had been the one to knock me out. He was lying, right? Greco was lying."

Mark stopped walking and Emma realized how far away from the house they had gone. They had reached the forest line at the edge of her family's property.

"Emma, there's a lot I need to tell you." Mark said slowly. He was looking down at the ground, shifting his weight from one foot to the next.

Emma pulled her hand out of his. "Was it you?" She demanded, her eyes widening in shock. She couldn't believe that he would do something like that to her. Mark, her best friend. "Were you the one who hit me?"

"It was for your own protection." Mark defended himself, trying to keep her calm. "You weren't supposed to find out about any of this."

Emma's face crumpled. Hurt and confusion battled for dominance inside of her. Tears pricking at her eyes, she dropped Mark's hand as she backed away from the one person she had thought she could trust most.

"You should leave." She whispered. Looking at Mark she felt nauseated at the thought of what would have happened if those men hadn't ran away. Mark had left her unconscious and helpless in a back alley when dangerous men were right there in front of them. He could never have fought them off on his own…

124

A strange sound drifted on the breeze from inside the forest. Emma cocked her head to the side, trying to hear more clearly. She could sense…something. She wasn't sure what though.

Mark opened his mouth to respond. Emma held a hand up to silence him, flicking an annoyed glance at him before she turned and stared at the forest again.

"What is it?" Mark asked, shifting to put himself between her and the trees she was staring at.

"I don't know." Emma whispered. She sounded genuinely confused, and very distracted. "Something is happening in the forest."

Before she could say anything else something slammed into the tree directly in front of them with a loud crash. Emma squeaked as Mark turned and wrapped his arms around her, curling his body around hers and shielding her with his body. Emma had never felt so tiny in her life. His head tucked over hers and his shoulders and arms curved around her so she was completely enveloped in his hug. When the sound faded Mark pulled away and bent to look into her face.

"Are you okay?" Mark asked, holding her face between his hands.

Emma nodded. "Yeah, I'm fine. What *was* that?"

Mark turned his head to stare at the tree that had been struck, keeping one arm protectively around Emma. Branches snapped as something tumbled out of the tree, grunting as it fell. Emma's jaw dropped when she saw Jason land in a heap on the ground. Emma and Mark stared in shock, unmoving. Jason didn't see them as he pushed himself to his feet.

"You think that was funny?" He yelled to whatever had thrown him.

"Jason!" Emma called his name. Shock melted away into concern as she realized what had just happened to him. She stumbled forward a few steps, not sure whether or not Jason was really standing there or if she was just seeing things.

Jason jerked around. When he saw Mark and Emma his expression darkened. "Stay away!" He bellowed, waving them off before running back into the forest.

"What?" Emma stared after him. She looked over her shoulder to say something to Mark but he was already sprinting past her. "Stay there!" He yelled back at her as he ran.

Emma's jaw dropped as she watched his retreating back. With a frown she snapped her mouth closed. "Yeah, like that's going to happen." She muttered as she started running after him. Mark had already disappeared into the forest before Emma could even take a few steps. "And since when could he run so fast?"

CHAPTER NINE

Mark sprinted into the forest and immediately heard the sounds of two people fighting. Angling in the direction of the fight he kept running and about 20 yards into the woods he stumbled into a small clearing. Loraine and Jason stood facing each other, so focused on the other that neither of them noticed Mark enter the clearing.

Flames sprouted from Jason's hands as he threw fireballs at Loraine. Every fireball he threw Loraine waved aside or knocked into the ground with her telekinesis. Jason paused too long between his attacks and Loraine took advantage of the gap to hit him with an energy blast. Jason went flying backwards and hit the tree Mark was standing next to. Mark looked at him and raised an eyebrow.

"Need some help?" He asked drily.

Jason looked at Mark suspiciously from where he had landed on the ground.

"What are you?"

"A Fighter." Mark replied. "Enhanced abilities."

"Great." Jason grunted, pushing himself to his feet. "A glorified gymnast."

Mark crossed his arms over his chest. "Big talk from a human lighter."

"I don't need help." Jason snarled, dodging another telekinetic blast from Loraine. "Get out of here before you get hurt."

Mark smirked. "I'm tougher than I look."

"I would hope so." Jason muttered under his breath, conjuring fire in his palms.

"Are you ladies finished? Hot head and I were in the middle of something, and I don't like being ignored." Loraine cut into their conversation. She flicked her hand at Mark, sending him flying to the right. Jason started unloading fireballs at her, so fast they were almost impossible to see.

Emma burst into the clearing just in time to see Mark land in a heap a few feet away from her. With a strange sort of shock she saw Jason with fire streaming from his hands as Loraine laughed. Unable to process what she was seeing Emma focused on the one thing she could understand, that Mark had been hit and was still on the ground.

"Mark!" Emma cried, running towards him.

Emma saw Mark's face turn into one of alarm as he looked past her. Jumping up he grabbed Emma, tucking her against his chest as he turned and crouched, shielding her with his body as the fireballs that Loraine were deflecting hit them. Emma blinked, confused. A light blue glow covered her body and Mark's as well, and it seemed to be deflecting the flames. In a sudden movement, Mark spun them out of the line of fire and behind a tree, tucking Emma between his chest and the tree trunk.

Emma felt her heart pounding against her chest. She waited to feel Mark patting at her head and checking her for burns but his hands stayed planted on the tree on either side of her. Emma blinked and looked up. Mark was staring around the tree, looking at someone. His gaze glanced somewhere else, then his eyebrows lifted.

Scooping Emma up into his arms Mark leapt out of the stream of fire and into the cover of the forest. Mark sped off, flashing through the forest at an impossibly fast speed around the clearing until he was near the trees behind Loraine. There Mark gently set Emma on her feet.

Gently setting Emma on her feet, Mark gripped her shoulders between his hands and looked her in the eye, blocking her gaze of the fight still going on between Jason and Loraine. Emma tried to look around him but Mark gently grabbed her chin and forced her to look at him.

"Em, I need you to listen to me." He said.

Emma nodded her head but her eyes flickered to the side for a moment. Her concentration was still on the fight.

Holding back a growl, Mark said quietly. "I'm going to carry you up this tree and put you someplace safe. You need to stay very still and don't move from that spot. I will come get you when the fight is over."

Emma looked up at the tree he had indicated and she frowned. "Mark, the nearest branch is fifteen feet off the ground. There's no way I could get up there."

"Don't worry about that." Mark brushed her argument aside. "Just don't move once we get up there. Understand?"

When Emma nodded Mark quickly threw her over his shoulder and secured her legs against him with one arm. Then he gathered his legs beneath him and jumped, landing on the lowest branch for just a fraction of a second before he jumped to the next branch. Within seconds Mark and Emma were 50 feet off the forest floor.

"I need you to slide off my shoulder now." Mark said calmly when they settled on a thick branch.

Emma's arms were locked in a death grip around his chest, her face buried in his back. When he said that she squeezed her grip tighter and shook her head furiously, refusing to open her eyes.

"It's okay Em, I've got you." Mark said, gently tugging at her leg.

"Are you insane?" Emma snapped. "I'm going to die. I don't want to die by falling out of a tree!"

"You're not going to fall." Mark said patiently. "Emma, this is important. I need to go help Jason but I can't do that if you won't let go."

Emma's grip loosened a little bit at the mention of Jason. Finally, with a whimper she released her hold and let him slide her off his shoulder. Mark gently placed her on a branch and she immediately wrapped both of her arms around the tree.

"I'll be back for you as soon as I can." Mark said, brushing a loose strand of hair from her face. "Just stay still and don't make a sound."

"Be careful." Emma whispered, looking absolutely terrified.

Mark smiled. Emma looked like a terrified kitten caught in the tree with her arms wrapped around the tree so tightly her face was pressed against it and her fingers dug into the bark. "I will."

Mark jumped from that tree to the next tree. Climbing around the trunk Mark looked for the sturdiest branch he could find. He spotted a thick one just above his head that reached out into the clearing and he climbed up to it. He climbed out as far as he could before his weight started bending the branch. Then he crouched down and waited.

Emma thought she was going to have a heart attack and she wasn't sure if it was from being stuck in a tree fifty feet in the air, Mark crouched on a branch suicidally far from the tree, or Jason fighting Loraine, who was looking more and more like a deranged demon. Jason was throwing fireballs faster than Emma could keep track. Loraine managed to deflect most of them but Jason was throwing them faster than she could keep up with.

A few of the fireballs found their mark, causing Loraine to stumble back a step or two. The smell of singed skin filled the air. The more Loraine struggled the fiercer Jason became. A few times Loraine knocked Jason to the ground. Instead of weakening him though his fire burned even brighter than it already was. It was as though the angrier Jason became the more fuel the flames had. It took everything in Emma not to cry out when Jason was hit. She didn't know what Mark's plan was but she didn't think giving away her location would help.

"You just can't find good help these days." Emma could hear Loraine taunting Jason. "Where did your friend go? For a guy who looks so big and intimidating he ran away really quickly."

Jason dodged a blast from Loraine and the bush behind him took the brunt of the attack. Dirt flew into the air as the bush was torn apart from the assault. Emma whimpered and clung to the tree tighter.

"How's this for big and intimidating?" Jason growled. His eyes began to glow as the fire on his hands and arms glowed even brighter. Between his hands he created a fireball four times the size of the others. Sweat broke out on his face as he tried to control it.

Loraine tried to hit him with a kinetic blast but the energy he was putting into the fireball kept him grounded in place. With a roar he threw the fireball at her. Loraine tried to block it but the force of the hit knocked her back five feet.

As Loraine struggled to her feet Emma saw that she was directly underneath where Mark lay in wait. With a jolt Emma figured out what Mark's plan was and she felt as if she had been doused in ice cold water. Mark launched himself out of the tree into a dive.

Emma felt her heart stop as she watched her best friend plummet towards the ground. She wanted to scream but her lungs were frozen in fear. A few feet above Loraine Mark curled forward, tucking out of his dive. Emma watched in shock as Mark slammed his foot down on the point between her neck and shoulder. Loraine crumpled to the ground, unconscious, and Mark landed with a roll.

Down in the clearing Mark stood up and brushed his hands off, nudging Loraine with a foot to make sure she was unconscious as Jason walked over to him.

"I think you and I need to talk." Jason said, stopping in front of Mark and crossing his arms over his chest.

Mark stood up to his full height and looked down at Jason. Jason wasn't a short guy by any means but Mark still towered above him. "Great idea. Let's talk about how long it took you to put her in position." He said, slowly crossing his arms over his chest as well. They stared at each other, sizing the other up in a silent challenge. Just then Emma's voice floated down from the tree Mark had left her in.

"Mark?" She yelled questioningly.

Jason raised his eyebrows at him.

"You left her in a tree?" Jason asked, a smile tugging at his lips.

Mark glanced at the tree in question, keeping his expression unreadable. "She has an unusual ability to get into trouble. It was the best I could come up with at the time."

"Mark!" Emma yelled again. Her voice was definitely not amused.

"I should probably go get her." Mark said, dropping his arms and stepping back from Jason.

A few seconds later he walked back into the clearing carrying Emma in his arms. Emma had her face buried in Mark's neck and her hands gripped his shirt so tightly that her knuckles were white. Jason chuckled when he saw the twigs and leaves caught in her hair.

"Is she okay?" Jason asked Mark as he approached.

Mark looked down at Emma. "She told me to get her down immediately but I think the 50 foot drop freaked her out a little."

"A little!" Emma yelped, raising her head from its hiding place. "I thought I was going to die!"

"You weren't going to die." Mark said, rolling his eyes. "I had you."

Emma's face flushed red. She pushed against Mark's chest angrily and screeched. "Put me down!"

Mark gently put her down and Emma stumbled a few feet away from him and Jason.

"One of you needs to tell me what is going on right now!" She said, her voice a little hysterical. "What are you?"

Jason looked at Mark in confusion. "She doesn't know?" He asked.

Mark glared at Jason. "No, she doesn't. I was just about to tell her when you got yourself thrown into a tree."

Jason whistled. "This should be fun to watch." He grinned broadly and waved for Mark to continue.

Mark turned to Emma who had her arms folded across her chest defensively.

"Em," He said gently, taking a step towards her.

Emma stumbled back a step. "Don't get any closer to me." She snapped, holding up a hand to halt him. "Not until you tell me what you are and what's going on."

Mark blew a breath out in frustration, pushing a hand through his hair. "Okay," he said slowly. "I guess I owe you an explanation."

132

"You guess?!?" Emma yelled at him. "You're my best friend, you should have told me you aren't human!"

"I *am* human." Mark said defensively. Emma narrowed her eyes at him in a death glare. "Sort of." He amended sheepishly. Jason chuckled in amusement and Mark turned to scowl at him but Jason just gave him an innocent look, twiddling his thumbs.

Mark turned his back on Jason to refocus on Emma. "You know all those movies and stories about vampires, werewolves, and people with special abilities we like to make fun of? They aren't completely fictional." Mark said carefully, watching Emma closely for her reaction.

Emma blinked, her face losing color. "You mean there are actually vampires?" Her voice sounded strangled.

"No no, there aren't actual vampires." He rushed to reassure her.

Jason snorted. "That's a matter of opinion." He muttered

Mark glared at him. "Shut up. I'm trying to keep this simple. She's already overwhelmed."

"What do you mean there aren't 'actual' vampires?" Emma asked, a little bit of color returning to her face. She still looked suspicious though.

"There are shape shifters who can do the whole bat thing and sometimes they like messing with Normal's heads. It's kind of a game with them." Mark explained, his expression disapproving. "For the most part we try to keep our abilities a secret. You weren't supposed to find out that people like us exist."

Emma looked at Jason. "There are more of you?" She asked in disbelief.

Jason nodded his head. Emma looked back at Mark.

"So what are you? Mutants or something?" Emma asked.

Mark shrugged. "Mutants, superheroes, demigods. Different cultures have their own names for us. Everyone's powers are different, just like the people they belong to."

"What are your powers?" Emma asked.

Mark looked uncomfortable. "Enhanced abilities." He said.

Emma's eyes narrowed. "What does enhanced abilities mean?"

"It means your boy here is faster, stronger, and has heightened senses than normal, even for our kind. He's basically a really cool pet, like a gorilla." Jason cut in. Mark glared at him, his muscles flexing under his shirt.

"I'm getting a little tired of you insulting me." Mark growled, facing off with Jason. "You want to test my powers for yourself? You could use a lesson in respect."

Jason grinned, anticipation for another fight shining in his eyes. "And I think you need obedience training. You aren't very good at following orders, pet."

Emma stepped forward to stand next to Mark, placing a hand on his arm to get his attention. Looking up into his eyes she shook her head slightly. Mark grumbled and shot a dirty look at Jason but he eased out of his aggressive stance.

"Good boy." Jason said approvingly. "You have him well trained Emma."

Emma glared at him. "I was doing you a favor." She said bluntly. "It's pretty obvious your ability has to do with fire." She commented, looking him up and down. "No one could be as hot headed as you without it affecting their powers."

Jason grinned at her, flames leaping from his hands again. "Generate and manipulate fire." He told her, twirling the fire around his hands until it was in the shape of a spinning hoop.

Emma jumped a little bit when his hands first burst into flame but then she seemed intrigued by the shapes he created with the fire.

"Stop showing off." Mark snapped. "What were you doing here and why were you fighting Loraine?"

The fire disappeared as quickly as it had appeared. Jason raised an eyebrow at Mark's commanding tone but he answered anyways.

"I was going for a run through the woods." Jason replied smoothly. "I saw Loraine sneaking around, thought it was suspicious and came to check it out. Next thing I know I'm being thrown into a tree."

"She just attacked you for no reason?" Emma asked, her expression shocked.

134

"Did she ask you about Tyler White or the journal?" Mark cut in, ignoring Emma's question.

"How do you know about Tyler White?" Jason asked, suddenly suspicious.

"Loraine and I have had our own run in. The accident after Chris Millers party wasn't an accident." Mark said. "She wanted me to tell her where Tyler was."

"Wait." Emma grabbed Mark's arm, forcing him to pay attention to her. "Loraine caused our car to crash? I had to take a class on reckless driving because of that accident!" Emma said with a huff. "How did she know we wouldn't die?"

Mark looked at her. "She didn't. At least, she didn't know you wouldn't die."

Emma's jaw dropped. "She didn't?" Emma said in a strangled voice. She pressed wrapped her arms around her stomach. "I think I'm going to be sick."

Mark reached out to stroke her hair reassuringly but Emma shifted out of his reach. Blood had drained from her face and Mark watched her in concern.

"Why would she think you would know where Tyler is?" Jason asked, turning back to Mark.

Mark never looked away from Emma as he answered. "Because until this year I've been the only person living here who has abilities. She thought I might be his contact or something."

"Did you tell her where he was?" Jason asked.

"No," Mark said bluntly, finally looking at Jason, "but I think they found him anyways."

"Wait, they have Tyler? How do you know?" Jason asked.

"Emma stumbled across three men in an alley torturing him two nights ago. I got there just as they were attacking her." Mark explained.

Jason turned to Emma. "I need you to tell me exactly what happened that night." He ordered. When Emma didn't respond he grabbed her arm, shaking her. "Emma!" He snapped. "Tell me what happened!"

Mark growled and pushed Jason away from her. He stepped in front of Emma, who was quickly blinking as she came back to reality. "Never grab her like that again." He said in a deadly voice. "This is the only warning you will get." Jason narrowed his eyes at Mark but after a tense pause he nodded. Mark crossed his arms, his jaw setting at a stubborn angle. "Before we tell you anything else you need to tell me why you are in Riverdale."

There was a brief pause as Jason and Mark stared at each other for a moment, sizing each other up.

"The Blade sent me." Jason said finally. Emma sensed Mark stiffen at the name. She glanced between him and Jason curiously. She had no idea who he was talking about but Mark was not happy to hear his name. "Someone in this town will be a lynchpin in the coming events. Our influence needs to be here."

"Did he tell you who?" Mark asked quietly.

Jason shook his head. "No."

A little of Mark's tension eased when Jason said that.

"Who is The Blade?" Emma asked curiously.

"He is a very dangerous man." Mark replied.

Jason glared at him. "He is doing what needs to be done!" He snapped, taking an aggressive step forward.

"Right and I guess you know all about what needs to be done." Mark snapped back, stepping forward as well.

Emma squeezed her way between the two of them and placed her hands on their chests. The top of her head barely reached their shoulders.

"Stop it. Both of you." She ordered, looking back and forth between the two of them. Jason and Mark continued to glare at each other for a moment before Mark turned away in frustration, stomping a few feet away. Jason smiled down at Emma, a slight twist to his lips that did nothing to lighten the darkness in his eyes. Emma dropped her hand and quickly stepped away from him.

"Sorry about that." He apologized. "We get just as passionate about politics as normal humans."

Emma let her hand drop from his chest. "You have politics?" She asked.

"In a way." Jason said vaguely. "But you said you saw three men torturing a man named Tyler?" He asked.

136

"A few nights ago." Emma said. "I was leaving work when I heard something in the alley behind the buildings. They were asking him about a journal. He wouldn't tell them where it was."

"What happened then?" Jason asked.

"They started torturing him so I tried to stop them." Emma began to explain but Jason interrupted.

"You tried to stop them?" He asked, shock written across his face. "Three dangerous men torturing a man you've never met and you tried to stop them?"

Emma blushed. "I know, it was stupid but I couldn't just stand there while he was being hurt!"

Jason just stared at her, shock, awe, and horror shifting through his expression.

"I don't know if you are brave, or just incredibly stupid." He finally said.

A faint growl came from where Mark had stalked off to. He was standing with his back to them, arms crossed, annoyance pouring off him in waves. Emma sighed and shook her head, turning back to Jason.

"Anyways," Emma said, continuing her story. "They tried to attack me but they couldn't hurt me. Then Mark showed up and knocked me out." Emma paused to glare at Mark's back. "He fought them and they ran off, taking Tyler with them."

"Why would they attack you?" Jason asked. "You're just a girl, you're not dangerous to them."

"Because Tyler called her Alexandra." Mark said, finally turning around. "Greco was there and he heard."

The blood drained from Jason's face and he stared at Mark in shock. "He's going to be coming after her." Jason said, looking at Emma.

Mark glared at him. "I know."

"Wait, if they don't have the journal yet then they are still going to be looking for it." Jason said.

"And if they find it then we're all screwed. I know." Mark said impatiently.

"We have to get Tyler back." Jason said.

"No," Mark said bluntly. "That would be suicide. My job is to protect Emma, not try to take down Drake's second hand man. What *you* have to do is call The Blade and get him to deal with this mess."

"Drake who?" Emma asked. "And what do you mean it's your job to protect me?"

Both of the guys ignored her as they continued their conversation.

"You won't be able to protect her if Drake gets control of the artifacts." Jason snapped. "They don't know where the journal is yet. If we can rescue Tyler he can take us to the journal and we can make sure it gets delivered to the Enforcers."

"First off, there is no way in hell I would do anything to help The Blade. And secondly, since you work for him why don't you tell him what's happening? I'm sure he would be very interested in getting involved." Mark pointed out.

Jason clenched his teeth together in frustration but he didn't say anything.

Mark looked at him curiously. "You do work for him...don't you?" He prodded.

Jason's face flushed red. "Of course I do!" He snapped. "I'm just...taking a break."

"No one takes a break from the Enforcers." Mark said with a laugh. "Not unless..." Mark's eyes widened in shock. "You were kicked out, weren't you?"

"Fine! If you won't help me I'll do it myself!" Jason snarled, turning and stalking off.

"Getting killed won't accomplish anything!" Mark yelled at his back.

Emma let out an ear-piercing whistle. Jason froze where he was. Mark winced and rubbed his ears.

"Both of you need to stop arguing with each other. I have no idea what is going on but from what I can tell neither of you want Drake getting his hands on this journal. So for right now you are on the same side." Emma said. Jason and Mark both grumbled and glared at each other. "Jason is right, we do need to rescue Tyler. But..." She said, holding up a hand to stop Mark's protest.

138

"Mark is also right, getting ourselves killed won't help anyone. That's why we are to do this the smart way."

Jason grinned in amusement. "And what exactly is the smart way?" He asked.

Emma stared at him. "I have no idea." She said, as if that should be obvious. "You two are going to have to play nice and figure it out. I think we should start out with finding out where they are keeping him though." Emma said.

A few feet away still lying on the ground where

Mark had left her Loraine began to move, slowly waking up. Emma grinned. "And she's going to tell us."

CHAPTER TEN

Emma, Mark, and Jason stood around a bound and unconscious Loraine.

"When is she going to wake up?" Emma murmured to Mark.

Mark looked at her with a wry expression. "Bored already?"

Emma wrinkled her nose at him. "No." She said quickly, swatting at the air. "But the mosquitoes out here are eating me alive."

"You could always go home and leave this boring interrogation stuff to us." Jason goaded her, fighting to hold back a smirk.

Emma's expression darkened. "I'm fine." She muttered.

After tying her hands, Jason and Mark had moved Loraine so she was sitting on the ground leaning back against a tree. Emma looked down at the unconscious girl and felt a pang of sympathy.

"Don't." Mark's voice cut into her thoughts. "She has tried to kill all of us and is working for someone who wants to hurt you. She is not worth your pity."

"Quiet." Jason hushed them. "I think she's waking up."

Loraine shifted on the ground, moaning quietly. Her eyelashes fluttered open and when she saw the three of them she jerked, trying to move her arms.

"Good morning sunshine." Jason said sweetly. "Sorry, about your hands. They're a little tied up at the moment but we have a few questions for you."

"And what makes you think I'm going to answer them?" Loraine sneered. She stared at Emma, eyeing her up and down. For a moment a slightly shocked expression crossed her face but then she covered it with her customary sneer.

Emma suddenly became aware of how much of a mess she was with twigs and leaves in her hair and dirt all over her clothes. She fidgeted under Loraine's stare, tugging her shirt straight and pulling the loose twig from the front of her hair.

Mark leaned towards Loraine, drawing her attention away from Emma. "Because if you don't Jason is going to take you to The Blade to be interrogated. So you either tell us now, or you tell him later." His deep voice was calm but his eyes shone with anger.

Loraine's face turned white at the mention of The Blade. She dragged her terrified stare from Mark to Jason. "You know him?" She whispered.

Jason nodded his face serious. "Yes, I do. And I've seen what he does to Drake's minions when they are careless with their powers."

Emma watched Mark and Jason as they spoke to Loraine. Their faces were dead serious and for the first time she saw how dangerous they were. Shocked, she realized that as she looked at them they appeared to have two layers. Their surface image, which was how she had always seen them before, and then there was a second layer.

Emma watched entranced as she stared at Jason. She could see flames flickering in his eyes and his skin glowed like fire flowed in his veins. He looked like fire personified and just like looking directly into a fire Emma found herself being mesmerized. Dragging her gaze away from Jason she looked at Mark and saw a difference in his appearance too.

While Jason's appearance was dangerous and entrancing, Mark's was overwhelming. He towered above her and his muscles pressed against the shirt that had once been loose on him. Mark's eyes caught every twitch Loraine made, every heartbeat, how her eyes dilated. Emma saw his ears twitch at sounds she couldn't even hear and she knew without a doubt that there wasn't anything in their vicinity that had escaped his notice.

"What do you want to know?" Loraine whispered. She still looked terrified at the thought that Jason would take her to this mysterious man called The Blade. Emma was becoming even more curious about who this man was and why his name would have such an effect on someone like Loraine.

"What were you doing in the woods?" Mark asked.

"I was sent here to capture Emma." Loraine replied sullenly.

"Who sent you?" Jason cut in.

"Greco." Loraine said. She looked at Emma with a smirk. "If Greco is after her than you might as well give up now. He always gets what he wants."

"Not this time." Mark snarled. "Where were you supposed to take her?"

Loraine hesitated and looked at them suspiciously. "If I answer your questions how do I know you won't turn me over to The Blade anyways?" She asked.

"I promise you we won't." Mark replied steadily.

"You promise? That means almost nothing to me." Loraine sneered.

"Maybe you'll like this one more." Jason said, flames bursting out along his hands. "If you don't tell us what we want to know I promise I will personally make sure that you burn the entire way to the Enforcer's encampment and once there that you receive the treatment we normally reserve for only the worst offenders. Do you believe that promise?"

Loraine looked at Jason's flaming hands nervously. "There's a cabin thirty minutes drive out of town up in the mountains. Greco told me to take Emma there."

"Is that where they are keeping Tyler?" Jason asked.

"I don't know." Loraine said, shaking her head.

"Where else could they be keeping him?" Mark pressed.

"I don't know!" Loraine snapped.

"If you don't have any good information for us then there is no need for us to uphold our end of the bargain." Mark said, standing up. "Jason, call The Blade and tell him we have one of Drake's spies." He said, nodding at Loraine.

Jason stood up and reached into his coat pocket for his phone. When he started to dial Loraine called out. "Wait!"

"Wait for what?" Jason asked, his finger hovering above the call button.

"I can't tell you for sure where they are keeping Tyler but I overheard Greco telling Ethan to go get chains and other equipment to take with them into the mountains. If they're not in the cabin then they are probably somewhere close to it." Loraine said, her words tumbling over each other in her haste to tell them what she knew.

"How many men are going to be at the cabin?" Mark asked.

"I don't know." Loraine said. "Greco, Ethan, probably a few of Greco's Elites. Greco didn't take many men on this trip, it was supposed to be a quick snag and back to the manor. Things got complicated when they found out Tyler had hidden the journal."

"I bet they did." Jason muttered.

Mark looked at Emma and Jason. "I need to talk to the two of you." He said, motioning away from Loraine.

The three of them gathered in a circle out of earshot of Loraine.

"I don't think we're going to get any more out of her." Jason told Mark.

"I agree." Mark looked back at Loraine. "But what are we going to do with her now? We can't let her go, she would only run off and warn Greco that we are coming."

"What about sending her to The Blade?" Emma said, looking at Jason. "It sounded like he would be able to handle her."

"No," Jason replied, his expression closed. "We can't involve him in this."

"Why not?" Emma asked. "I thought you worked for him?"

"I do, but in this case it would be best to handle it ourselves." Jason replied evasively.

Mark eyed Jason suspiciously but Emma just shrugged.

"So what do you think we should do with Loraine then?" Emma asked him.

Jason frowned in thought. "We could keep her at my place until we rescue Tyler." He said. "I have a basement we can keep her tied up in. After the rescue we'll let her go but until then she needs to be kept locked up."

Mark looked thoughtful. "That might work." He said. "Do you have the right set up for keeping someone there?"

Jason nodded. "A few minor adjustments may need to be made but it shouldn't be a problem."

Emma cut in. "Are you guys listening to yourselves? You are talking about kidnapping someone and holding them captive! What if she has parents who will be worried about her?"

Mark shook his head. "Loraine is living on her own here, just like Jason is. The only one who will be missing her is Greco."

"Which means we will have to move quickly before he suspects she was captured." Jason said.

"But…" Emma said.

Mark held up a hand to silence her. He tilted his head to the side, listening to something Emma couldn't hear. Then he looked back at Emma.

"Your mom is calling for you." He said. "Go back home, stay there for the rest of the day. Jason and I will take care of Loraine. Tomorrow you and Jason need to go to school and act like everything is normal. We'll all meet up tomorrow night and figure out our next move."

"Are you serious? You just expect me to go home and pretend like nothing happened?" Emma asked. "After finding out that there are people running around with super powers and I'm at the top of a bad guys most wanted list you're telling me to go home and go to school tomorrow like everything is fine?"

Mark looked at her. "Yes." Was his blunt reply.

When Emma opened her mouth to argue he cut her off. "Look, I know it's a lot to take in but it's really important that you do what I say. I'll explain more tomorrow but for now just go home."

144

Emma looked at Jason for support but he just shrugged. Emma glared at Mark and stormed off in the direction of her house.

"Emma, wait!" Mark called after her. With a huff Emma turned around. "What, Mark?" She demanded, propping her hands on her hips.

"Don't leave your house tonight." Mark warned.

Emma glared at him, but when he gave her a stern look she turned and stormed off.

That night Emma sat in her room and stared out her window. The house had gone to bed hours ago. No lights were on and the air was absolutely still. Emma wished she could sleep as easily as everyone else. She had tried to go to sleep hours ago but everything that had happened that day kept circling in her head, keeping her awake.

She hadn't been imagining things when she had seen Greco torture a man with just a touch or when the knives the knife wielder had been spinning suddenly disappeared. Those men had powers like Mark and Jason. *Don't leave your house tonight.* Mark's words floated across her thoughts. Did Mark really think she was in danger? Loraine had caught them off guard but Mark and Jason had been able to handle her easily. Maybe she wasn't in as much danger as they thought.

Even as she tried to convince herself that was true a voice inside her head told her it wasn't. Loraine had just been the first move. Greco couldn't have known that Jason and Mark would be there to protect her. If Emma had been by herself Loraine would have had no problem catching her. Emma realized how vulnerable she was. She couldn't count on Jason or Mark always being there to protect her. What would she do if Mark and Jason weren't there and she had to defend herself?

The thought made her frown. She had never been a fighter, she was more the type to turn the other cheek type. Or to trip over her own feet as she stumbled backwards and make a complete fool of herself. But in this case when turning the other cheek meant being captured by a dangerous man for who knows what purpose...putting up a fight was probably a better idea.

The thought of being captured made her think of Tyler. The image of his face when he had seen her flashed through her mind. He had looked stunned to see her and then he had panicked when he thought they were going to catch her too. He had called her Alexandra though. Emma frowned. Was it just coincidence that he had thought she was someone named Alexandra or had Tyler known Alexandra Savage?

The thought send Emma scrambling from her seat next to the window and running over to her closet, digging the box out from where she had hidden it. Pulling out the diary Emma curled up on her bed and began searching through it for any mention of Tyler. After skimming through entries for half an hour she finally found something.

April 3, 1990
Dear Diary,
Today I met Tyler White. He is very unusual for someone from the White family. He seems actively interested in what is happening, especially with my brothers. When I asked him why he was so curious he wouldn't give me a straight answer. I think he knows something about my brothers. Their family has all the records of our kind, including prophecies. If there is one in there about my brothers I have to find out.

There was nothing in the rest of the entry about Tyler. Emma sat back on her bed, dropping the diary in her lap. Tyler had definitely known Alexandra. That might be why he had called her Alexandra that night, maybe he had thought she looked like her? It seemed like a stretch but crazier things had happened recently.

Just then Emma yawned so hard her jaw popped. The exhaustion hit so quickly she could barely keep her eyes open long enough to drop the diary on her bedside table before she fell asleep.

The next day Emma stood in front of her locker, still thinking about everything she had learned last night. She was just putting her books away when Amy tracked her down.

"Emma!" Amy said, suddenly appearing next to her. "What happened this weekend? We were supposed to go dress shopping on Saturday but when I called your mom said something had happened and you needed to stay home. Did you get in trouble or something?"

Emma hesitated for a moment before remembering the story Mark had told her mother.

"I stumbled across a couple of muggers beating a man up Friday night after work." Emma told her. "I tried to help him and one of them knocked me out. Luckily, Mark ran up and scared them off before anything happened. I'm really sorry I missed shopping with you, I was sleeping most of Saturday."

Amy's face looked horrified as Emma told her what had happened. When Emma finished her story Amy threw her arms around Emma.

"I'm so glad you're okay!" She exclaimed. "What were you thinking trying to stop a mugging by yourself? You could have been hurt!"

Emma laughed. "I know, I know." She said, peeling Amy off of her. "Kathryn already gave me that speech."

"Never do anything like that again!" Amy told her, going back to their conversation. "You're going to give me a heart attack! First an impossible to survive car accident and now starting a fight with a couple of muggers, you are either the luckiest girl I know for still being alive or the most unlucky for having these things happen to you."

Emma smiled at her friends concern. "Let me know when you figure out which one it is." She said with a wry expression.

Amy nodded and looked at the clock in the hallway. "I have to go." She said apologetically. "I just wanted to make sure you were okay."

"I'm fine." Emma reassured her friend. "There isn't a scratch on me."

Amy gave her one last hug before turning and disappearing into the crowded hallway. Emma shut her locker and turned to go to class, almost walking directly into Jason who was standing directly behind her. She jumped a little before glaring at him.

"Stop that." She snapped, pushing past him.

"Stop what?" Jason asked, his voice confused as he turned to follow her.

"Appearing out of nowhere right behind me. It's freaky." She told him.

"I don't think it's the fact that I manage to sneak up on you all the time that's freaking you out, because Amy just did the same thing about five minutes ago and you didn't snap her head off for it." Jason pointed out.

"Maybe I like Amy more." Emma glared at him. "What do you want, Jason?" She dodged around a group of friends standing in the middle of the hall, a small part of her hoping Jason would get stuck behind the crowd.

"Why are you acting like you're mad at me?" Jason demanded brusquely, pushing through the crowd after her.

"I'm not mad at you." Emma said shortly, speeding up a little.

"Please," Jason said sarcastically. "You are practically running away from me. Is this about yesterday?"

"You mean finding out that you are some sort of fire throwing mutant?" Emma replied equally sarcastic. "Or how much of a jerk you were to my best friend?"

Emma heard Jason swear under his breath but she didn't dare to look back and see how frustrated he was. She could see the door to her classroom, if she could just get in there Jason would have to drop the conversation.

Hope was beginning to spark in her chest when a strong hand latched on her arm and Emma was nearly yanked off her feet. Jason dragged Emma out of the main hallway into an empty side hall that led to the janitor's closet before she could even voice a protest. He pinned her against the wall and bent down until he was looking her in the eye.

"I know this has all been a sudden shock for you and I'm sorry for that." Jason said quietly. Emma could see flames flickering in his eyes, his temper was dangerously close to the surface. "But whatever emotions you might be feeling right now you need to get over it because there is more going on here than you know about and you are quickly getting drawn into the middle of it. Our kind has one cardinal rule: Don't let humans know we exist. If you break that rule you will be held accountable for it and neither Mark nor I will be able to protect you. Do you understand?"

148

Emma nodded, more than a little afraid of Jason at that moment.

Jason's eyes searched hers intently for a moment. Then he leaned back, apparently realizing that he was scaring her. "I'm sorry, I know you didn't ask for this but I'm going to try to help you as much as I can. You just need to trust me, okay?"

Emma nodded again, but it was a pacifying gesture. Trusting him was not something she was willing to do yet. She wanted to ask him what he had meant when he said there was more going on than she knew but before she could form the words a shadow fell over both of them. Morgan stood in the entry of the hallway, staring at them in disbelief.

"What is going on here?" Morgan hissed. She was so angry Emma could almost see sparks coming out of her eyes.

"Emma and I were just talking." Jason said, stepping away from Emma. Emma remained plastered to the wall. A small part of her hoped that if she was still enough she would blend into the wall and they would forget about her.

"It didn't look like you were just talking to me." Morgan snapped. Fury radiated off of her in waves. For a second Emma was afraid she would attack them right then and there.

Jason walked towards her. "Well, we were." He said bluntly. "Now if you'll excuse us, we need to go to class."

Morgan stepped aside to let Jason pass. It was either that or let him push her aside. When Jason stood in the hallway he looked back at Emma and arrogantly motioned for her to follow him. Moving slowly, Emma peeled herself off the wall and crept out of the hallway, cringing at the fury in Morgan's eyes. As Emma walked past her Morgan grabbed her arm, fingers digging cruelly into Emma's skin.

"You're going to pay for this." She hissed in Emma's ear. "If you don't stay away from him you are going to become a social pariah here. You'll never have any friends again. Even Amy won't want to talk to you anymore."

Jason frowned and came back to where the two girls were standing.

"Morgan." He said warningly. "Let her go. Now."

Morgan held her grip on Emma's arm for a moment longer before letting go. Flipping her hair over her shoulder Morgan strutted off, her nose in the air as the crowded hallway parted before her. Jason's hand settled on the small of Emma's back as he guided her through the hallway towards their class. Emma was too shaken to protest. Thoughts of all the ways Morgan was going to kill her paraded through her head.

"What did she say to you?" Jason demanded. He looked angry again. Even knowing his anger wasn't directed at her Emma felt herself shrink away from him. Jason looked down at her with a frown. Emma looked around and noticed she wasn't the only one scared of him. A path was opening before them in the crowded hallway as other students stumbled to get out of Jason's way as he led Emma to class.

"The usual." Emma said with a shrug, her fear of Jason lessening as they continued to talk. " 'Don't mess with me or I will ruin your life.' Normal Morgan stuff."

"Does she say things like that to you often?" Jason growled.

"On a daily basis." Emma replied. She watched as a large football player who had a reputation for being a bully warily eyed Jason up and down before shifting out of the way. "I've never seen her that mad before though."

Just then Emma realized that Jason's hand was still on the small of her back. She frowned and moved away from him. "I appreciate your help with Morgan but I'm still not happy with you either."

Jason raised his eyebrows and a look of grudging respect entered his eyes. "I'm sorry I lost my temper back there." Jason apologized, letting his hand drop. Emma searched his face, inwardly sighing in relief when she saw no hint of anger in his expression. "But you can't go shouting this stuff around. People are either going to think you're crazy or it's going to attract unwanted attention to both of us and right now we have other things we need to be focusing on."

"Fine." Emma said as they stopped in front of Mr. Schneider's classroom. "I will keep your secret, but it's going to take me a while to be okay with all of this."

Jason nodded. "I know, it's a lot to take in all at once. I wish you hadn't found out the way you had."

Emma stared at Jason for a moment. His blue eyes were like chips of ice and his strong jaw was clenched tight. His face looked like it was chiseled from granite it was so harsh and unforgiving and yet he was still so handsome. It made her heart hurt to see all the anger and bitterness in his eyes. He still scared her a little but she was inclined to believe he was telling the truth and that he might actually want to help her. Emma nodded reluctantly and walked into Mr. Schneider's class with Jason right behind her.

CHAPTER ELEVEN

At lunchtime Emma wandered into the cafeteria, not really paying attention to anything happening around her. She hadn't heard any of the lectures her teachers had given her or even what the homework for the night was. Too many thoughts crowded in her head, each one of them just as distracting as the others.

It had probably been a mistake to come to school today. So far nothing good had happened. Kathryn hadn't wanted her to go anyways, she thought Emma was still shaken up over the mugging incident. Emma smiled ironically, Kathryn didn't even know the half of it.

Despite her distraction Emma couldn't help but notice people staring at her as she walked by and the whispering that followed her as she walked towards where she and Amy normally sat. Emma looked around, trying to convince herself that she was just being paranoid but the other students were definitely staring at her.

A table full of girls quickly looked away when Emma's gaze fell on them as she walked past. Emma wondered if they somehow knew what had happened last night, like the truth was stamped on her forehead for the world to see. Emma shook her head. No, there is no way anyone could know that there were people with super powers running around. She was just imagining things. When Emma came into sight Amy waved her over to their table frantically.

"Hey Amy." Emma said, dropping her new mini cooler lunch bag on the table and sliding onto the bench. "What's up?"

Emma noticed a group of freshmen at the next table staring at her. She glared at them until they all looked away, but as soon as Emma turned to talk to Amy whispering exploded behind her.

"Did you actually make out with Jason in the janitor's hallway before school?" Amy whispered excitedly, leaning towards her so other people wouldn't overhear their conversation.

"What?" Emma yelped. The freshmen at the other table looked over at her again. A few of them even shifted closer to try to overhear Emma's conversation with Amy. Emma glared at them again, lowering her voice to whisper like Amy. "No! Who told you that?"

Emma looked around the cafeteria and noticed more than a few people watching them.

"It's spreading around school." Amy replied, glancing around as well. She looked nervous as she fiddled with the silver bangled bracelet she was wearing that day. "What were you thinking? You know Morgan is going to be furious about this."

"I didn't do anything!" Emma whispered furiously, ducking her head to avoid all curious looks. "He pulled me into the hallway because we needed to talk about something, that's it."

"What did you need to talk about?" Amy asked. "I thought he freaked you out." She was staring at Emma with her big blue eyes, giving Emma the kind of look that made it so easy to want to tell her things. Amy was her best friend, if Emma could tell anyone it would be Amy. Emma opened her mouth to tell her everything that had happened when she caught Jason staring at her from across the room. His eyes were intense as they watched her, as if he knew exactly what she was about to do.

Emma sighed and looked back at Amy.

"I can't tell you." She said apologetically, her shoulders slumping.

Amy looked at her with a hurt expression. She and Amy had never kept secrets from each other before, they had always told each other everything.

"You can't tell me, or you won't tell me?" Amy asked quietly. Emma squirmed in her seat, guilt spiraling through her.

"I can't." Emma said. "If it was just about me I would tell you," She added quickly, "but other people's secrets are involved and they trust me not to tell anyone what I know."

Amy stared at her for a moment longer before nodding her head. "If you say you can't tell me then I guess there must be a really good reason."

Emma smiled in relief but Amy still looked worried.

"What is it Amy?" Emma asked.

Amy looked at her carefully, watching Emma's reaction to her next question. "You would tell me if you were in trouble, wouldn't you? Because if you need my help you know all you have to do is ask."

Emma smiled and gave Amy a big hug. "I know you would and it means a lot to me that you would say that even though you don't know what is going on. I'm fine. I just promised someone that I wouldn't tell anyone his secret and I can't break my promise."

"His secret?" Amy's eyes lit up. "Is it Jason? Does he have some big secret that he doesn't want anyone to know?"

"I think that would count as me telling you their secret." Emma said with a laugh. "I can't tell you whose secret I am keeping and please don't try to figure it out."

"Okay fine." Amy said a little put out at not being told a big piece of gossip. "But you're still going to have to deal with Morgan. I don't think she will care what you and Jason were doing, everyone in school thinks there's something going on between you two now. You know she can't just let that go."

Emma got a sick feeling in her stomach. When it came to revenge Morgan was ruthless, Emma had seen it first-hand many times. Emma jumped to her feet and grabbed her lunch.

"I've got to go." She told Amy.

The doors to the cafeteria burst open and Morgan came storming into the room, followed by her two closest friends, Heather and Hannah. Her face was flushed and her eyes practically spat sparks as she searched the room, her anger so strong it was almost palpable. Everyone in the room fell silent, staring at the terrifying image that she made.

154

"You!" She said when her eyes settled on her adopted sister. She plowed her way through the crowd, pushing unfortunate bystanders out of her way as she charged at Emma. "How dare you humiliate me like this! When I get my hands on you, I swear I'll kill you!"

Emma jumped up from her seat and held her hands out in front of her. "Morgan, wait! It's not what you think! There is nothing going on between me and Jason!" She said quickly, trying to reason with her.

"Nothing is going on between you two?" Morgan screeched. "I saw you with him this morning! Everyone in school knows what you did!"

"No! We're just friends, I swear!" Emma said. She dodged around a table as Morgan got closer, trying to put as many obstacles between them as she could. Wherever she went people scattered, not wanting to get caught between Morgan and Emma.

"Liar!" Morgan screamed. "You've had a crush on him from the very beginning! Everyone knows you like him!"

"But it's never been like that between us, we're just friends!" Emma said, running around another table as Morgan ran around the first one.

"Morgan!" Jason's voice cut through the commotion and suddenly the crowd parted to show Jason racing towards them. "Stop it!" He commanded as he ran up to stand between the two girls.

"Oh, are you protecting her now?" Morgan snarled as she tried to circle around Jason towards Emma.

"She didn't do anything wrong." Jason snapped, blocking Morgan from getting past him with his hands. "We were just talking."

"That's not what I saw!" Morgan yelled, trying to find a way past him. "And that is not what the entire school has been saying all day."

"The entire school is wrong!" Jason told her. "And so are you!"

Jason stayed in a defensive position, shifting to keep Morgan in front of him and away from Emma. Emma stood a few feet behind him, watching the scene unfold with wide eyes. The rest of the students had formed a circle around them and they were watching the drama like they were watching a modern day version of the gladiator games. Suddenly Emma realized yet again that she was letting someone else stand up for her instead of fighting her own battles.

"Jason, get out of my way right now or it is over between us!" Morgan yelled, giving up on trying to get past him.

The room grew even more silent as everyone held their breath waiting for Jason's reply. Losing his defensive posture Jason stood up straight and looked at Morgan with disdain.

"It never should have even began with us." He said coldly.

With a shriek of fury Morgan shoved him into a group of football players. Caught off guard Jason stumbled back and the football players grabbed him, restraining him from interfering as Morgan charged at Emma.

Emma just stood unmoving as Morgan ran towards her, her eyes wild and her face twisted in anger. She watched as if from a distance as Morgan's fist came towards her face, but she didn't move.

The blow, when it landed, knocked Emma off her feet and she fell on the cafeteria floor. Emma felt heat spreading across her cheekbone where she had been hit but there was no pain. Emma reached up with one hand and rubbed the side of her face, surprised that it didn't hurt.

"You are worthless, you pathetic waste of life!" Morgan yelled at her. "Your parents didn't want you, my family doesn't want you, and no one else is ever going to want you either."

At the mention of her parents Emma's brain refocused. With that focus came the anger that she always held back and she realized that she was no longer scared of Morgan. This was the worst that Morgan could do and Morgan had nothing left to scare her with.

Emma casually stood up as if falling on the floor had been a part of her plan all along. Ignoring Morgan who was continuing to shout insults Emma calmly straightened her clothes and brushed the dirt off. When Morgan circled around to insulting Emma's parents again Emma looked at Morgan with deadly intent in her eyes.

"Shut up."

Morgan's words stumbled to a halt as she looked at Emma in shock. Her mouth gaped open but words seemed to escape her as she stared at Emma.

"Jason and I never kissed." Emma said, loudly enough for everyone to hear. "And even if we did, how could you get mad when you've been kissing every guy in school?"

Emma heard gasps in the crowd and people started murmuring. Morgan looked around at the crowd surrounding her, realizing for probably the first time that Emma knew all of her secrets and now she was going to tell them to everyone.

"Shut up." Morgan hissed at Emma.

"What's wrong Morgan? You don't want people finding out all of your secrets? Like how you flirt with your teachers to get them to give you better grades? Or maybe how you sabotage all of your "friends" relationships so that none of them have a boyfriend to keep you from having their undivided attention?"

Off to the side Morgan's two best friends jerked when they heard that. Their eyes narrowed as they looked at Morgan. If looks could kill Morgan would have been dead at that moment.

"She's lying!" Morgan yelled, looking at her friends. "I would never do that to you!'

Heather and Hannah just looked at her coldly before they turned and walked away without giving Morgan a second glance. Around them the crowd started getting louder as more and more stories about Morgan began being told.

Emma stepped forward until she and Morgan were face to face.

"I am not scared of you, Morgan." Emma said quietly, "And if you so much as dare to even mention my parents again you will be the one to walk away with a black eye."

Then Emma turned and walked away, leaving Morgan alone in the middle of the crowd. Jason met Emma at the edge of the crowd.

"You okay?" He asked, looking at the eye Morgan had punched.

Emma nodded and kept walking. She just wanted to get away from the crowd and somewhere she could breathe. Pushing open the doors that led from the cafeteria to the common area in the middle of campus Emma walked out, Jason following her. When the doors shut behind them the noise of the crowd was cut off and Emma took a deep breath of the fresh air, slowly beginning to relax.

She and Jason wandered over to one of the benches scattered around the common area and sat down. The concrete was cold and as Emma stared at the overcast sky she began to shiver.

"Here." Jason said, pulling off his coat and draping it around her shoulders.

"Thank you." Emma said, smiling shyly. She tucked the coat around her, ducking her head between her shoulders and pulling the collar up over her neck.

"So was what you said true? Has Morgan really done all those things?" Jason asked. His eyes looked sad, as if he already knew the truth but he wanted to hear it from her anyways.

Emma dropped her gaze from his. "Yes." She said softly.

"Why didn't you say something?" Jason asked. He leaned forward, bracing his elbows on his knees and clasping his hands loosely in front of him. He didn't look at her when he asked but she knew she had his full attention.

"I guess I didn't think you would believe me." Emma replied.

She watched as a squirrel ran across the grass and scurried up a tree, chattering angrily at another squirrel that had followed it up.

"I would have rather heard it from you then hear it announced in front of half the school." Jason said, giving Emma a crooked smile.

"I'm really sorry." Emma said, pulling the coat tighter around her shoulders. "I didn't think about how it would affect you. I was just so mad at Morgan."

"It's okay, I understand." Jason said with a shrug. "Do you have any other big secrets that affect me that you think I should know?"

Emma pretended to think about it for a minute before leaning towards him and whispering. "I don't want to freak you out but...you shoot fire from your hands."

158

Jason gasped, looking shocked. "What? I do!" He said, placing a hand dramatically on his chest.

Emma nodded gravely. "It's true. I'm sorry I have to tell you like this but…you should know."

"Thank you." Jason said gratefully. "You are a good friend."

"I try." Emma said with a playful grin.

"Alright little Miss Keeper of Secrets, let's get you home before someone else tries to start a fight with you." Jason said, standing up and offering Emma a hand up too. Emma laughed and let him pull her up.

"But it's so much fun being punched in the face!" Emma said in exaggerated enthusiasm.

"Oh I know from experience how much fun it is." Jason said with a laugh.

The two of them began walking to the building where Emma's locker was so she could go get her things, neither of them seeing Morgan as she escaped from the angry crowd in the cafeteria. Morgan watched with hatred in her eyes as Emma and Jason walked away.

Kathryn was incredibly understanding when Emma called her to tell her she was going home. Emma told her that school had been too overwhelming and she had experienced a minor panic attack when she got crushed in the crowded hallway. She told Emma that after such a traumatic event it was perfectly normal to need some time to readjust. So Emma spent the rest of the afternoon hanging out in her room watching television. Kathryn had meetings with clients until four that night so Emma was home alone when the doorbell rang at 3:00.

Emma opened the door, slightly surprised to see Jason standing on her doorway. He looked as darkly handsome as ever, wearing a black jacket over his fitted grey shirt and dark wash jeans. Emma tugged self-consciously at her over-sized comfy t-shirt and sweats. Her hair was thrown up in a messy bun and she knew she looked like a total scrub. Jason looked her up and down, noticing every detail of her appearance.

"Okay, let's go." He said abruptly, turning to leave.

Emma blinked in surprise. "Excuse me?" She said. She didn't make any move to walk out of the door, she just stared at Jason when he turned back to look at her impatiently.

"We're meeting Mark at my house." Jason said patiently, as if Emma should have already known about this.

Emma paused, waiting for him to explain more. When Jason didn't say anything else Emma decided to prompt him. "Why?" She said slowly.

"To talk about the Loraine situation." Jason replied, equally slowly. "Come on, let's go." His voice was suddenly brisk again. He tried to reach through the doorway to grasp her arm but Emma shifted out of his reach.

"Dressed like this? No way." Emma said, shaking her head adamantly.

Jason gritted his teeth in annoyance. "Then change." He replied curtly, crossing his arms.

Emma sprinted up the stairs and Jason yelled up after her. "You have five minutes!" Eight minutes later Emma jogged down the stairs, wearing a nice pair of jeans and a cute top.

Emma paused in the entryway to check her hair, before grabbing her purse from the entryway table.

"Okay, I'm ready!" She announced, stopping in front of Jason.

Jason looked at her curiously. "You don't care if I see you in sweats but as soon as I mentioned going to see Mark you ran off to make yourself look cute? Is there something going on between you two I need to know about?"

Emma rolled her eyes exaggeratedly. "No!" She said, drawing the word out. "I never leave the house in my sweats. You never know who you'll see."

"Yeah." Jason agreed sarcastically, turning to walk out the door. "You might see Mark!"

Emma followed Jason in her own car as he drove to his house on the other side of town. Since they were keeping Loraine in Jason's basement they had decided that it would be a good idea if Mark stayed there during the day to keep an eye on Loraine until they were ready to let her go. They didn't want Loraine to escape

160

and warn Greco that they were going to try to rescue Tyler. When Emma had asked him what they were going to do with Loraine after they had rescued Tyler he had just shrugged.

Pulling up to Jason's house Emma was surprised with how normal it looked. It was a small box house, one story from what she could see but Jason had mentioned that it had an underground basement. The house was painted white with a blue trim that looked like it was in need of repainting. The yard was a small square of dying grass that was mottled green and brown. The two windows at the front of the house had the curtains closed so no one could see inside. All in all it was very plain and unremarkable. She was a little disappointed, she had been expecting something a little more like a super hero lair. Instead Jason's house was a small place on the outskirts of town, not really nice but not dumpy either. It was so normal that no one would look twice at it.

Parking in the small driveway Emma got out of her car and followed Jason to the front door, managing to trip over a tuft of grass growing through a crack in the concrete as she did. Opening the front door Jason paused for a moment and turned to look back at Emma, who quickly straightened up. Emma blushed a little when Jason raised an eyebrow at her.

"Don't mind the burn marks." Was all he said before turning and walking inside.

Emma looked at the mundane doorway suspiciously. Curious as to what he meant Emma followed him, pausing on the threshold as she looked inside. The front door opened into a small entryway with the living room on the right. The living room was small, it had a couch, a lazy boy and a television. Straight back from the front door was the kitchen that Emma only caught a glance of through the doorframe. In the little area next to the kitchen and the living room was a small table with four chairs around it that didn't look like it was used very much.

Emma looked back at the living room, taking more notice of the furniture in it. The couch and the armchair both looked old and well worn. The leather was faded and scratched in areas but the cushions looked deep and inviting. It made Emma think of her favorite pair of old tennis shoes, they didn't look like much but nothing was more comfortable. In front of the couch and the armchair was a beat up coffee table. Sturdy wood, plain design, it was made for kicking up your feet and relaxing.

In fact, the only things Emma could see that weren't old and beat up was the television and the stereo system. The television was a nice 40 inch LED flat screen that looked like it was new. Next to it was an impressive stereo system set against the wall. Emma didn't know enough about stereos to know if that was a good brand or not but she could tell that it was expensive just by looking at it. A very complicated looking universal remote lay on the coffee table within easy reach of the couch and the armchair. Emma shook her head. Boys and their toys.

"Are you coming in?" Jason asked, pausing to look back at her.

Emma nodded and stepped into the house as Jason walked into the kitchen.

"Do you want anything to drink?" He called back to her from the kitchen. "I have water, soda, orange juice and milk."

"Water would be great." Emma replied.

Now that she was inside she began seeing scorch marks on the wall and on the couch. Emma wandered a few steps into the house, tracing her fingers over one of the scorch marks on the wall. The wallpaper had bubbled from the heat in some places. Emma poked at one of the bubbles experimentally but the wallpaper had hardened up again.

Losing interest in the wall Emma wandered over to the living room. Emma smiled as she trailed her fingers over the back of the couch, a little surprised by how soft and smooth the brown leather was. The trashcan next to the couch was empty except for the melted remains of another universal remote exactly like the one currently on the coffee table.

Snagging the melted remote from the trashcan Emma walked into the kitchen where Jason was getting them drinks. Jason pulled his head out of the refrigerator holding a bottle of water in one hand and a soda in the other.

"Here you go." He said as he turned, pausing when he saw Emma holding up the remote.

"What happened to this?" Emma asked teasingly.

Jason scowled and put the soda down on the counter before snatching the remote from her hand. "Nothing." He said, tossing it in the trashcan underneath the kitchen sink.

"Really? Did it spontaneously combust?" Emma asked skeptically.

162

"No." Jason replied darkly, handing her the water bottle.

"Thank you." Emma opened it and took a sip. "So what were you watching that got you so mad you melted the remote?"

"It isn't just anger that causes me to randomly start shooting flames." Jason told her, grabbing a cup from the cupboard. "Adrenaline does it too."

"Okay," Emma replied, leaning against the counter. "So what were you watching that got your adrenaline pumping?"

"I was watching an action movie, and the good guy was fighting the bad guy but he kept making stupid mistakes and he got his butt kicked." Jason said, grabbing ice from the freezer to put in his cup. "The girl he was trying to impress saw the whole thing. The whole fight scene I kept thinking about what I would have done instead and how I would have beaten up the bad guy." Jason looked down at his hands for a moment before opening the soda and pouring it into the cup. "I guess I just got really into the movie. Anyways, the next thing I know I'm holding another melted remote in my hands."

"Another?" Emma asked. "Does this happen often?"

Jason shrugged. "Usually about once every other month. More during football season."

"Jason? Is that you?" Mark's voice floated into the room.

Emma looked around, confused as to where he could be. Aside from the kitchen and living room there was a short hallway that led back to the bedroom and another door for the bathroom. The only other door in the hallway lead to what she thought was a closet but when Jason walked over and opened it she realized it was a stairway to the basement.

"It's me." Jason said. "Emma is here, too."

Emma heard footsteps stomping up the stairs and seconds later Mark walked into the kitchen.

"Emma!" He exclaimed when he saw her. "What happened to your face?"

Mark rushed to the refrigerator and grabbed an ice pack, hurrying back to gently press it against her eye. Emma wrinkled her nose and leaned back, taking the ice pack out of Mark's hand.

"I'm fine, Mark. Really." She said, touching her slightly swollen black eye.

"Relax, Mark." Jason said, putting a hand on Mark's shoulder and pulling him away from Emma. "It's just a black eye."

Before Emma could tell Mark what had happened he whirled around and grabbed Jason, picking him up by the front of his shirt and slamming him into the wall a few inches off the ground.

"You said you'd keep her safe." Mark's voice was deadly soft. Emma froze. She had never seen this side of Mark before. He looked like he seriously wanted to hurt Jason.

"Mark!" Emma yelled. "Stop it! Put him down right now!"

Jason gripped Mark's forearms with his hands and stared Mark in the eye, completely calm. "Let go of me." He warned.

Mark shifted his grip, pulling Jason away from the wall and slamming him back against it, even higher.

"Mark, put him down!" Emma snapped. "It was just stupid school drama. I'm fine!"

Mark ignored her, keeping Jason pinned against the wall. Jason's hands burst into flames, burning Mark where his hands were gripping. Mark never blinked, never looked away from Jason as his arms were burned. He shifted his grip again, sliding one hand up to wrap around Jason's throat, sweat sprouting on his forehead as Jason's fire flashed hotter.

"Jason, stop! Both of you knock it off!" Emma yelled, running over to them. Pushing against Mark's shoulder with one hand she tried to yank Jason's hand off of him with the other. Flames danced in Jason's eyes. He was completely lost to the fire within him. His head turned so that his flame filled eyes regarded Emma. Slowly the flames began to creep up his arm to where Emma gripped his arm.

CHAPTER TWELVE

Before Emma could even react to what was happening Mark released Jason, dropping his right hand and following through with an elbow to Jason's face. In the same movement he spun, scooping Emma up and carrying her into the kitchen away from Jason. Dropping her in the corner of the room Mark turned to face Jason, ready to fight if he attacked. Jason shook his head, the fire slowly disappearing from his hands as he rubbed his jaw.

"Look at me." Mark commanded when the fire was gone.

Jason looked up, his eyes a clear blue again.

"You good?" Mark asked.

Jason nodded.

For a second everyone in the room stood perfectly still. Mark and Jason still stood staring at each other, neither one of them wanting to be the first person to move. Finally it was Emma who inched her way around Mark so she wasn't trapped in the corner anymore.

"Are you okay?" She asked softly, looking down at the holes burned into the sleeves of his shirt where Jason's hands had been.

Mark nodded once, his eyes never leaving Jason's.

"How bad is he burned?" Jason asked, staying where he was.

"I'm not sure." Emma said. She looked up at Jason, who had the shuttered look of a man who knew he had done something wrong but didn't want to admit to his mistake. "Do you have scissors and anything for burn injuries?"

Jason nodded. "I'll go get them." He said, disappearing down the hallway.

Mark relaxed a little bit when Jason was out of sight, finally looking down at Emma.

"Are you okay?" He asked, capturing the hand that she had used to pull at Jason and inspecting it for burns.

"I'm fine." Emma said, tugging her hand out of his grasp. "You need to sit down so I can take care of those burns."

Mark shook his head. "Don't worry about it. They will heal."

"Humor me." Emma said dryly. "Now sit down."

Mark gave in to Emma's urgings and sat down at the table just as Jason walked back into the room.

"Here are the scissors." Jason said, handing them to her. "And this is the burn ointment and some gauze to wrap around the burns."

"Thanks." Emma said, setting each of the items on the table next to Mark.

"What are the scissors for?" Mark asked, looking at the scissors suspiciously.

"I need a clear look at your burns and your shirt is ruined. I figured it would be least painful if I just cut the sleeves of your shirt off just above the burns." Emma replied briskly, picking up the scissors.

Mark frowned. "I really liked this shirt." He said. Mark looked over Emma's head at Jason. "You're buying me a new shirt." Mark told him as Emma began gently cutting the sleeves just above the burn marks.

"Oh hush," Emma chided him. "You have a million shirts like this one, and to be fair you did attack him first."

"Maybe next time he'll remember not to bring you back with a black eye." Mark said. He frowned at her. "How exactly did you manage to get a black eye?"

166

"Maybe next time you'll ask questions like that first before you attack me." Jason retorted.

Emma shot a glare at him before turning back to Mark and cutting the sleeve off of his other arm. "Before school started Jason pulled me into a side hallway to lecture me about how important it is that I keep everything I know about the two of you a secret. Morgan saw us and wasn't too happy about it. Apparently someone else saw us too, by lunchtime everyone was talking about how Jason and I had been making out in the side hallway."

Emma quickly recounted the whole fight scene to Mark, keeping her eyes focused on applying the ointment to his arms, ending with. "So I announced a few of her secrets out loud for everyone to hear and now I'm pretty sure she has no friends because of me."

Emma slowly looked up, not sure what Mark's reaction was going to be. Mark was grinning from ear to ear, looking prouder than a parent whose child just took their first steps. When Emma was finished applying the ointment he slapped her on the back. "Finally!" He exclaimed. "I've been waiting for you to stand up to Morgan for years! I'm glad she finally got what she deserves."

Emma shook her head as she wound the gauze around Mark's arms. "I'm not proud of what I did." She said. "No one deserves to be publicly humiliated like that. I just lost my temper when she said my parents didn't want me. Not that it's much of an excuse."

"Hey," Jason spoke up, "You stood up for yourself and that is something to be proud of. Morgan has been bullying you for years, you don't need to feel bad for her."

"That's right." Mark said. "Morgan needed to learn that she can't keep treating you like her own personal punching bag."

Emma put the gauze down on the table and leaned back in her chair, looking back and forth between Mark and Jason.

"So will one of you explain to me why Jason attacked me?" She said matter of factly, changing the subject.

Jason shifted uncomfortably and looked away, his expression ashamed. Mark was the one who answered Emma.

"Elemental powers like Jason's can be very difficult to control." Mark told her, leaning back in his chair too, careful not to

167

brace his sensitive arms against the armrests. "They tap into the primitive side of the user, so sometimes when they are being attacked they begin to react by instinct instead of thought. When you grabbed Jason's arm his instincts registered it as another attack and so he reacted."

Emma's mouth formed an O as she processed what Mark was saying. She looked up at Jason. "Does that always happen?" She asked.

Jason was leaning against the wall a few feet away, his arms and legs crossed. He shook his head. "No, not always. Usually I can keep control of it but sometimes if I'm surprised or my emotions get too strong it will."

"What I can't figure out is how you weren't burned." Mark said. He grabbed Emma's arm again as if the burn might have showed up while she was bandaging his.

"Wait, was she burned?" Jason asked, jolting upright. His face was horrified as he stared at her. "Emma, I am so sorry!"

Emma shook her head. "No, I wasn't burned." She said. "Don't feel bad, I'm fine."

"That's what I mean." Mark said, talking to Jason. "I saw her hand engulfed by the flame. She should be burnt."

Jason looked confused as well. "I've never known anyone to be immune to my fire." He said. "Did you feel anything Emma?"

Emma shook her head slowly. "No, not really." She said. "I was too busy concentrating on trying to get you two apart."

"You were so busy concentrating that you didn't notice your hand going up in flame?" Jason asked skeptically.

Emma glared at him. "Mark reacted so fast I didn't even know. He had me halfway across the room before I even realized you had tried to burn me."

"This wasn't the first time your flames haven't hurt her either." Mark told Jason. "When we were fighting Loraine, she deflected a string of your fireballs at Emma. I tried to shield her but the flames didn't even hit me, something blocked them."

Jason looked at Mark curiously. "You mean, that wasn't you?" He asked. "I assumed you were the one throwing up the shield."

Mark shook his head. "Shielding isn't one of my powers."

Emma pushed her hair back out of her face. This conversation was going nowhere. Suddenly Mark grabbed her hand, staring at her bracelet.

"Emma, where did you get this?" He asked quietly. Jason leaned over her shoulder, trying to get a look at what Mark was staring at.

"I found it when I was cleaning out the attic a few weeks ago." Emma told him.

"Before Chris Miller's party?" Mark pressed. He was staring intently at the symbols on the bracelet, tracing them with one of his fingers.

"Yeah." Emma said.

"Can you take it off?" Mark asked her. "I want to have a closer look at it."

"Uhhhh, not exactly." She hedged.

"What do you mean, not exactly?" Mark stared at her suspiciously.

Emma shrugged and pulled her arm out of Mark's grasp. Propping her elbows on the table she played with the bracelet, rubbing her thumb on one of the metal disks. "It's kind of a crazy story." She said.

"Start from the beginning." Mark directed, leaning forward. Jason circled the table and sat in the chair across from Emma, bracing his elbows on the table and leaning forward as well.

Emma looked back and forth between them, suddenly feeling like she was in the middle of an inquisition. "I mean I don't really know how to explain it." She said.

"Try." Mark said firmly.

Emma blew her breath out in exasperation. "Okay fine. When I cleaned the attic I found a box of my parent's belongings. There were only a few things in the box, the bracelet being one of them." Jason and Mark exchanged a look when she told them that but they didn't say anything so she continued. "I didn't want anyone to know I had found the box though so I hid it in my closet and I didn't tell anyone that it was there."

Emma paused, not sure how to tell Jason and Mark the next part.

"So what happened next?" Jason asked.

Emma looked at him. "Remember that crazy guy that came into the coffee shop a few weeks ago?"

Jason nodded. "Yeah, I saw you wander off after him and Mark."

"Well...he kind of attacked me." Emma said. "Mark and I were talking to him and he just jumped at me, slamming a metal disk onto the back of my neck."

Jason scowled at Mark. "So much for keeping her safe." He muttered.

Mark scowled back at him.

"I noticed that the bracelet had a missing space when I found it." Emma said quickly, hoping the guys weren't about to start fighting again. "It looked around the same size so I tried to see if the metal disk I had gotten from Tyler would fit. A flash went off when I put the two together and I dropped the bracelet under the desk. When I reached under to grab it the bracelet sort of..." Emma motioned vaguely with her hands, blushing in embarrassment.

"Sort of what?" Jason asked.

"Attached itself to me." Emma finished lamely.

"Can you get it off?" Mark asked.

Emma shook her head. "No. I tried everything, nothing can break it!"

Mark nodded, his expression thoughtful. "And all this happened the night before we got into a car accident that the doctors said should have been impossible to survive." He said musingly.

"Do you think the bracelet caused the accident?" Emma asked, confused as to why he thought there might be a link between the two.

"No," Mark said, refocusing on her face. "I think the bracelet saved you."

170

Emma paused, waiting for Mark to start laughing and tell her he was kidding. But his face was totally serious.

"Seriously?" She said, her voice full of skepticism. "You think a bracelet saved me?"

"How is it that you're sitting next to a guy who spontaneously combusts and you find it hard to believe that a bracelet can have shielding qualities?" Mark's lips twisted in a wry smile as he leaned back in his chair.

"It's not spontaneous!" Jason said defensively. "…anymore."

"I don't know." Emma said. "I could just always tell you guys were different. This is just an old bracelet I found in the attic."

"Don't you think the timing is kind of convenient?" Mark asked. "You just happened to find a mysterious bracelet that attaches itself to you and is impossible to get off, right before what should have been a fatal car crash, a mugging attempt, and being fire blasted?"

"If it's a shielding bracelet then why didn't it protect me from Morgan?" Emma asked.

Mark hesitated. "I'm not sure." He said admitted. "Maybe it doesn't work around humans?"

"Then why were you able to knock me about when those men were attacking me?" Emma asked, pointing out another flaw in his argument.

Jason grabbed Emma's wrist, inspecting the bracelet. "I've heard of objects that bond to their user." He said quietly. "They react to what the user feels and what they want. Maybe this bracelet raises its defenses only when you feel like you're in danger. You trust Mark and you know Morgan would never seriously hurt you so it doesn't shield you from them."

Mark nodded his head thoughtfully. "That could explain it." He said. "But have you ever seen one of those objects for yourself?"

"Before now?" Jason asked, dropping Emma's hand and leaning back in his chair. "No, I don't know anyone who has.

They're just legends. But if this bracelet is one of them than it must be very powerful."

Emma heard a hint of awe in Jason's voice as he talked about the bracelet. She rubbed her wrist where he had touched her, pulling her hands back towards her chest.

"Are bracelets like this not very common then?" She asked.

Jason shook his head and looked at her consideringly. "No. In fact it is so valuable that there are quite a few men who would kill to get their hands on something like this."

Emma swallowed nervously. "Maybe I shouldn't be wearing it then." She said. "I don't want someone killing me for a bracelet."

"As long as you don't trust them no one will be able to touch you." Jason said. "And I can't think of anything that will do a better job of protecting you than this." He pointed at the bracelet.

"Wait, how do we know we can even trust this bracelet to protect me?" Emma asked. "I didn't exactly get it from a reliable source."

"It has so far." Mark commented. He never took his eyes off her face, measuring her expressions for what she was really thinking. "Besides, you said yourself you can't get it off. I don't think you have much of a choice until we figure out how to get it to unbind."

"You don't know how to get it off me?" Emma's voice squeaked a little as she said this. In the back of her mind she had assumed Mark would know how to deal with this. If he didn't then that meant...she really was stuck with it.

Mark shook his head. "I'll have to do some research and see what I can find out. Until then just be grateful it's a protective bracelet and not something worse."

Emma gave him a horrified look. "There are things that are worse?"

Jason snorted in amusement. "Oh yeah." He said, nodding his head exaggeratedly.

"Where are we at with the whole Tyler situation?" Emma said, changing subjects. She wasn't sure if she believed that her bracelet had shielding abilities and she definitely wasn't sure if she wanted to continue wearing it if it did. If it was something people would kill to get she didn't want to be the one standing in the way of them and what they wanted.

"Jason and I questioned Loraine last night." Mark replied. "She didn't tell us much more than what she said when you were with us. There's a cabin in the mountains where they might be keeping Tyler, besides that she has no idea. It's our only lead so far though so Jason and I are going to go check it out on Friday and do a little recon.

"What about me?" Emma asked. "Don't I get to go too?"

"No." Mark said, shaking his head sharply. "Jason and I have experience in this type of thing. Besides, you are going to be busy."

"Busy with what?" Emma asked.

"You will find out Friday." Mark told her.

Emma rolled her eyes. "Are you really not going to tell me?" She asked.

Mark grinned. "I'm really not."

"You're annoying." Emma told him. "So you two kept talking about a journal yesterday but no one has told me why it's so important yet."

Jason and Mark exchanged glances before Jason cleared his throat.

"Maybe we should talk about that later." He murmured, shooting Mark a look.

"Why not now?" Emma asked.

"Just drop it, Em." Mark told her.

Emma looked back and forth between the two guys but it was clear from their expressions that neither one of them were going to change their mind. Emma huffed in annoyance and slouched in her chair.

Silence fell over the room. Mark stared out the window and Jason stared off at nothing, both men caught up in their thoughts. Emma traced a finger on a pattern in the wood table. Emma looked at Mark out of the corner of her eye.

Emma spent a few more hours with Jason and Mark before she told them she had to go home for dinner. Kathryn had insisted that Emma be home for dinner every night that week. Emma wasn't looking forward to the scene that was likely to occur when she got home and had to face Morgan but there was no way she could avoid that. Mark volunteered to walk Emma out to her car, which was a little unusual but Emma had wanted to talk to him alone anyways so she didn't argue.

Emma and Mark didn't talk as they walked to her car. Emma kept thinking about how Mark had reacted when he saw her black eye and a traitorous part of her mind pointed out that guys only do that when they really care about the girl. Maybe he didn't just see her as a friend…

"Why did you attack Jason when you saw my black eye?" Emma asked abruptly.

Mark shrugged. "You're the closest thing I have to a little sister." He said simply. "When a guy brings you back to me with a black eye I get a little over protective."

She was right, he didn't think of her as a friend. He thought of her as a little sister. Emma's heart sank.

"Just a little?" Emma asked dryly as they reached her car.

"Yeah." Mark said with a grin. He reached out with one of his giant hands and rubbed the top of her head, turning her hair into a mess. "Your face looks bad enough as it is, with an ugly bruise you're just a lost cause."

"Hey!" Emma squealed, ducking from beneath his hand. "Not the hair!"

Emma ran a few steps away from him, finger combing her hair back into place while she glared at him. "You can say I'm a lost cause but we both know I'm the better looking one of the two of us." She said, giving him her best stuck up Morgan look.

Mark laughed. "Lies." He said. Emma stuck her tongue out at him and dug her keys out of her purse. "Drive straight home." Mark ordered. "Don't stop anywhere."

Emma rolled her eyes and opened her door, pausing to look back at Mark. "You know saying that makes me want to find someplace to stop at, just because you told me not to."

"Emma." Mark said, his voice completely serious. "Drive straight home. I'm going to call you in ten minutes to make sure you got there."

"Alright fine, I'll go straight home." Emma said, annoyance dripping from her voice. "But for the record, I think you are taking this whole protective role a little far."

Mark chuckled. "As long as you go straight home that's fine."

When Emma got into the car Mark tapped on her window so she rolled it down.

"Yes daddy, I promise I'll drive safely and wear a seat belt." She said sarcastically.

Mark reached in and flicked her on the ear, startling a yelp from her.

"Go home after school tomorrow." He said. "You'll have a surprise for you."

Emma's eyes lit up. "A surprise?" She asked excitedly. "What is it?"

"Go home tomorrow and you'll find out." Mark said with a wink. He patted the top of her car and stepped back so she could drive away.

Pulling up at the house after school the next day Emma walked inside, noticing that nobody's cars were there. She must have beat Morgan home and Kathryn was probably out running errands. Emma wandered inside and checked to see if there were any packages for her lying around. Nothing. Emma sighed. Maybe Mark had just told her to go home to get her out of his hair. She could see him doing something like that. Wandering over to the kitchen Emma had just stuck her head in the fridge to see if she could find something to eat for an after school snack when someone rang the doorbell.

Emma looked curiously at the door. No one else was home so who would be coming over? Emma walked to the front door and slowly opened it.

"Emma!" Amy said cheerfully. "Great, you're home!"

"Oh, hey Amy." Emma said, opening the door wider and stepping back. Amy came bouncing through the door with a package in her hands, looking more excited than Emma had ever seen her. "I didn't know you were coming over." Emma said.

"That's because it was a surprise." Amy said with a big grin. "Well, actually it's part of the surprise, I haven't told you the other part yet."

Emma eyed her suspiciously. "There's another part to this surprise?" she asked.

Amy nodded emphatically. "Yep!" She said. "We're going shopping!!!" Amy bounced up and down, clapping her hands excitedly.

"Shopping?" Emma asked, her voice incredulous.

"Yes!" Amy was practically glowing with excitement. "We're driving to the city and we're spending the night shopping! Oh, by the way this is for you." Amy handed the package to Emma.

"Who's it from?" Emma asked, taking the package.

"I don't know." Amy shrugged. "It doesn't say on the front. But we are going shopping tonight and we are going to get you an entirely new wardrobe because…" Amy paused and looked Emma up and down. "Well sweetie, you really need clothes that fit. You look like a homeless person."

Emma tugged at her shirt self-consciously. "No, I don't." she said in a pouty voice.

"Yes, you really do." Amy said, nodding her head sadly. "But don't worry, after tonight you will have a whole new wardrobe that actually fits you! Now grab your things because we need to leave if we want to get there on time." Amy said briskly.

"Get there on time? You mean we're on a schedule?" Emma asked as Amy herded her towards her bedroom.

"Of course!" Amy exclaimed. "What do you think I've been doing all day? I've been busy planning this out so we can get the most accomplished in the time we have. We only have one night after all. That's a lot of shopping to cram into just a few hours."

"Oh no." Emma dropped her head forward and groaned.

"Hush, you're going to love it." Amy chided her, shooing Emma upstairs. "And even if you don't you're going to thank me tomorrow when you have all your new amazing clothes to wear. Now go get your purse!"

Before she went back downstairs Emma dropped the package on her desk to open when she got home. Ten minutes later Emma was sitting in Amy's car listening to Amy gush about how much fun they were going to have as they drove towards the city.

While Amy and Emma drove south Mark and Jason were north of the town, just approaching the cabin Loraine had told them about. The mountains were only a thirty-minute drive from Riverdale but the guys had decided to park their car at the base of the mountains and hike the rest of the way. As Mark and Jason crept through the forest keeping an eye out for anyone patrolling the woods Mark's phone vibrated. Mark pulled out his phone and laughed quietly when he saw the text Emma had sent him. *I hate you.* Was all the text message said.

"Was that from Emma?" Jason asked quietly, coming up next to him.

Mark nodded and slipped his phone back in his pocket. "Yeah, Amy has picked her up." He said.

"Did she tell you she hated you?" Jason asked, looking at Mark's phone curiously.

"Oh yeah." Mark replied with a smile. He refocused on their surroundings then, pointing towards a break in the trees thirty yards from them. "That's the clearing where the cabin should be." He said. "I think we should both circle around the perimeter and check for guards, we can meet up on the other side and decide where to go from there."

"If there are guards should we avoid them or neutralize them?" Jason asked, his manner cool and professional.

"Avoid them, this is just a recon mission." Mark said.

Jason nodded and the two guys separated, Mark circling the clearing to the left and Jason circling to the right.

"What do you think about this?" Amy asked, holding up a light blue shirt. The material was light and airy, something that would be perfect now that the weather was warming up.

"That's cute." Emma agreed. Amy beamed and handed the shirt to the assistant who was helping them. The young woman took the shirt with a smile and walked away, taking it to the dressing room to hang up for Emma to try on when she was ready. This whole shopping spree had been like something out of a makeover fantasy. Amy had taken her everywhere, make-up stores, clothing stores, shoe stores, even to purse and perfume stores. It was the type of day most girls dream about. And yet Emma found herself wishing she was hiking around in the woods with Mark and Jason.

"Emma? Helloooo. Are you there?" Amy said, trying to get Emma's attention.

"I'm here." Emma replied, refocusing on Amy.

Amy propped her hands on her hips in a disapproving gesture. "I know you don't like shopping but can't you at least pay attention? You seem like you're a million miles away right now."

"I'm sorry Amy, it's not that this isn't fun, I guess I'm just really distracted." Emma said, feeling a little bit guilty. Amy was doing all this to help her and Emma wasn't exactly acting grateful.

"Distracted I am used to," Amy said, somewhat mollified by Emma's apology. "This is something entirely different though. What's been going on with you lately?"

"Nothing important." Emma said, aimlessly flipping through one of the racks of clothes.

"Really? Because you went from being meek and mild to taking on Morgan in front of half the school in just a few weeks. I think there's more going on that just 'nothing'." Amy said, returning to browsing through clothes. "Although I am glad you finally used all the gossip I've been telling you about Morgan. I've been hoping you would eventually, although I thought you would use it as blackmail, not to make her the most hated person at school."

Amy smiled when Emma blushed and ducked her head. "I didn't mean to do that." Emma said in an embarrassed voice, "But when she brought up my parents I just lost my temper. She crossed a line and she knew it."

"I completely agree." Amy nodded. "But still, I feel like there is something going on with you that you aren't telling me."

Emma shrugged. "I don't know why. My life is just as boring and unexciting as ever."

"Except for this shopping trip, because this is amazing and exciting." Amy corrected. "What do you think about this?" She asked holding up a cardigan.

Emma scrunched her nose in distaste. "No, thanks."

Amy shrugged and returned the cardigan to the pile she had picked it up from. "So what has been going on with you?" She asked. "You can't tell me it's nothing because it obviously isn't. Is it Jason? Is something going on with the two of you?"

"What?" Emma exclaimed, looking up from the pile of clothes she had been searching through. "No! Of course not! We've just…become friends, I guess."

"Mmhmm." Amy said knowingly. "He was certainly quick to jump to your defense when Morgan went all psycho ex-girlfriend on you." Amy picked up another shirt and showed it to Emma. When Emma nodded her approval Amy handed the shirt to the assistant to take to the dressing room.

"Seriously Ayms." Emma said, wandering over to a new pile of clothes. "We're friends. He was just trying to help me out because he was the one who had pulled me into the hallway that morning."

"Alright fine," Amy giving up on that line of questioning. "Then is it Mark?"

"Amy!" Emma exclaimed in exasperation. She didn't want Amy asking her any more questions about Mark or Jason, her lying skills were definitely not good enough for that. Amy was bound to figure out something was up. "I'm not dating Mark or Jason, we're just friends."

"If it's not boys then what has been going on with you?" Amy asked. "You've lost weight, you're becoming more confident, and now you spend all of your time with two incredibly hot guys. Something had to have caused all of that."

Emma shrugged. "The weight loss is from running and I've always been friends with Mark. As for Jason, well that's just a weird situation that I don't even know how to explain. So nothing has really changed." She held up a pair of pants for Amy's approval. Amy nodded and Emma handed the pants to the assistant. When the young woman walked away Emma looked at Amy. "How many clothes do we have waiting in the dressing room?" She asked curiously.

Amy looked back in the direction the girl had gone. "A lot." She said simply. "You should probably go try some of them on before we run out of room in there."

Emma turned to walk to the dressing room and Amy called out after her, "Let me know if you find anything cute!"

CHAPTER THIRTEEN

Up in the mountains Mark and Jason had both circled around the perimeter of the clearing, meeting on the other side from where they had started. They crouched down between a large bush and a tree, out of sight of the cabin.

"Guards?" Mark asked in a whisper.

Jason shook his head. Mark nodded and pointed at the route he had taken, also indicating that he hadn't seen any on his side either. The only guards they had seen were two standing outside the cabin door, but they didn't know if there were any inside the cabin. At least they knew this was the right cabin. The two of them crept forward, using the vegetation in the forest to stay hidden. At the edge of the clearing they stopped. Jason kept an eye on their surroundings as Mark inspected the cabin.

It was a simple structure, small, probably only two rooms. The cabin was directly in the middle of the clearing, only a small dirt road led up to it. Besides that the entire clearing was empty, nothing to hide behind or use for a shield. Two guards stood outside the door, and Mark could see another two through the cabin windows. The cabin looked like it had a basement that they were probably keeping Tyler in. If there was then there would be at least another guard or two down there with him. Mark tapped Jason on the shoulder and motioned for them to fall back.

The two of them snuck out of the area much quicker than they had entered and drove back to town.

Saturday morning Emma, Mark, and Jason sat around the small kitchen table at Jason's house. They were telling her what they had discovered on their recon mission to the cabin the night before. She smiled to herself when she remembered their reactions to her appearance when she had walked in the door. They had both just stared at her for a minute before either of them could think of anything to say. Jason had rushed to offer her something to drink and had pulled out her chair. Mark just looked at her like he didn't know who she was anymore. It took a few minutes and a lot of teasing on her part for them to relax around her again.

"Two guards by the door and one or two more inside." Jason counted off, holding a glass of orange juice in his hand. "Those odds aren't too bad. What do you think?"

Mark shook his head, frowning in concentration. "There's something off about all of this, it seems too easy somehow."

Emma leaned forward. "Four men of unknown abilities against the two of you seems too easy to you?" She asked in slight disbelief.

Jason spoke up. "No, he's right. It doesn't seem like there should be anything suspicious about this and yet there is."

Mark grunted in agreement, leaning back in his chair and crossing his arms over his chest. "It might be a setup, but who do they think would try to rescue Tyler? It was just Emma and me that night, for all they know Emma's just a high school girl who can shield herself. They wouldn't think she's much of a threat."

"Maybe they think The Blade found out he's been captured and they'll try to rescue him?" Jason said.

"If they were trying to stop a rescue attempt they would have more guards or move him to a better location. This feels like a trap to me. The question is a trap for who?" Mark said.

Jason hesitated. "You don't think it would be a trap for Emma, do you?" He asked Mark.

Mark and Jason both turned and stared at Emma, who slouched down in her seat. Finally Mark shook his head.

"They don't know anything about Emma except that she can shield and whatever Loraine told them, which wouldn't be much. I don't think they would expect her to go running to the rescue."

Jason just shook his head and took a drink out of the orange juice in his hand. Emma cradled a cup of coffee in her hands as she glanced back and forth between the two guys.

"So…what's the plan then?" Emma prompted.

"What do you mean?" Mark asked, staring at her in confusion.

"How are we going to rescue Tyler?" Emma persisted. "You have a plan, right?"

"Look, Emma," Mark said. "It's too dangerous. We don't know what we're up against. It would be stupid to go in there with no idea what to expect."

"We can't just leave him there!" Emma argued. "What happened to needing to get him away from Drake's men so they don't find the journal?"

"She's right." Jason said with a grimace. "We can't let them get the journal. There's too much at stake."

Mark growled in frustration. "So then what do you suggest we do?" He snapped at Jason.

"Hey, don't get mad at me." Jason said. "I'm just agreeing with Emma."

"If it is a trap then maybe they are trying to flush Emma out." Mark said. "They might not be expecting the two of us to show up. We might have a chance to catch them by surprise."

"I thought you said they wouldn't be interested in me." Emma reminded him.

"You, no. Your bracelet, that is a different matter." Mark replied.

Emma sat up, her eyes alert. "So does that mean we're going?"

Mark glared at her. "No." He said. "That means Jason and I are going. You are staying here."

"What? No!" Emma protested. "I'm not staying behind while you and Jason run off to be the heroes. I can help!"

"The only one you'll help is Greco by distracting Jason and I. If you are there we will be too worried about taking care of you, we won't be focusing on our mission." Mark told her.

Emma turned to Jason for support. "Jason, please let me come!" Emma begged.

Jason shook his head, his face serious. "Mark is right." He said. "You shouldn't come."

"But I can help!" Emma argued.

Mark stood up abruptly. "We said no, Emma. Now go home. Jason and I have a lot of plans to make before tonight."

"Tonight?" Emma said in a shocked voice, slowly standing up. "You're going tonight?"

"Yes." Mark said brusquely. "Now you need to leave."

"Let me go with you!" Emma exclaimed. "I could wait in the car."

Mark shook his head. "We aren't taking a car. We're riding dirt bikes up to the cabin."

Jason stood up too, but he made no move to help Emma as Mark herded her out the door.

"Mark, please let me stay." Emma pleaded as Mark opened the front door and walked her outside.

"I'm just trying to keep you safe." Mark said softly. "Everything will be okay. I'll let you know as soon as we get back tonight."

Before Emma could say anything Mark walked back inside and shut the door behind him.

The moon was high in the sky as Emma hiked through the forests of the Rattlesnake Mountains. Before Mark had kicked her out that morning Emma had seen where he had marked the location of the cabin on a map in the living room. As soon as she got home she had looked up the location and marked it on a map of her own so she could follow them without being caught. There was no way she was going to let Mark and Jason risk their lives while she sat at home and did nothing. After an hour and a half of hiking Emma was grateful for all the morning runs she went on, there was no way she would have been able to hike this a few months ago. Now she knew why Mark and Jason had decided to take dirt bikes.

Emma paused to take a drink of water and check her location. According to her map she was almost there. Emma put the water and map away in the small hiking backpack she had brought and began creeping forward, her eyes and ears open for anyone that might find her. If Mark found her stumbling around in the dark he would send her home immediately and Emma wasn't about to let that happen.

Continuing to creep forward, Emma finally reached the edge of the clearing where the cabin was. From her vantage point off to the left of the front of the cabin she could see the two guards by the door. Emma swallowed nervously. Mark had made it seem like it would be no big deal to get past them but now that Emma saw the guards for herself she wondered if maybe he had been trying not to scare her. The guards were absolute giants, even bigger than Mark. Emma would never try to take on one of them in a million years, much less two.

Just then Emma heard a *thunk* and the first guard crumpled to the ground. Before the second guard could even realize what had happened there was a second *thunk* and he fell to the ground as well. Emma held her breath as two shadows detached themselves from the forest and silently ran across the clearing towards the cabin. Mark and Jason were making their move. Reaching the cabin they burst through the front door. Emma could see them fighting two more guards through the windows of the cabin. She was so engrossed with what was happening in the cabin she didn't hear the sound of a branch snapping behind her. Emma's muscles tensed to run into the cabin to help Mark and Jason when everything went dark.

Mark dropped the body of the guard he had been fighting to the ground. Now that he and Jason were inside the cabin he could see the stairway that led to the basement. With a beautiful right hook Jason knocked the guy he was fighting out, dropping him to the floor as well. Mark caught Jason's eye and nodded to the staircase, motioning that he would go first. Jason nodded and the two of them crept down the staircase together.

The basement was just one big room with a cement floor and walls. No guards were in the basement, just Tyler. He was handcuffed to a chair in the middle of the room. His head was dropped forward on his bare chest and his hair was drenched in sweat. Mark didn't know what they had been doing to him but Tyler looked like he was more dead than alive. Running over to him, Jason worked on reviving Tyler while Mark set about breaking the handcuffs that were chaining him to the chair.

"Tyler. Tyler you need to wake up." Jason said quietly, shaking Tyler's shoulders.

Tyler slowly lifted his head. "Who are you?" He asked, his voice hoarse and scratchy. "What are you doing here?"

"We came to get you out of here." Mark said, coming around the chair to face Tyler.

Tyler's eyes brightened in awareness. "I remember you!" He exclaimed. "You were there the night she tried to rescue me."

"Yes, that was me." Mark said patiently. "Now can you stand up? We need to leave."

Tyler's face turned to panic. "Birds! Birds in a cage about to be clipped!" His eyes cleared for a moment and he grabbed Mark's arm. "You have to leave! She must be protected!"

"Who must be protected? Emma?" Mark questioned him.

"She is a Forgeron. She holds the key." Tyler whispered urgently.

Mark and Jason exchanged a startled glance.

Tyler grabbed the front of Mark's shirt. "Give this to her, when she is ready." He murmured, shoving a glowing gold orb into Mark's hand.

"A Memorex?" Mark studied the golden orb sitting in the palm of his hand.

A whisper of noise floated down the stairway. Mark and Jason tensed, listening intently for any other sounds that someone was there but all they heard was Tyler mumbling about birds and cages. After a moment Jason looked at Tyler's vacant expression then back at Mark.

"We don't have time for this." Jason growled impatiently. "Let's just grab him and get out of here."

Ducking under Tyler's arms, they half carried and half dragged him out of the room and up the stairs. Tyler kept babbling about a bird in a cage, his feet scrabbling uselessly against the ground. As the three of them stumbled into the main room the sound of a slow clap reverberated from the walls, freezing the blood in Mark's veins.

"Congratulations gentlemen." A cultured voice said. "You managed to free Tyler. Almost."

Mark slowly looked up. Greco stood in front of them, seven of his best fighters in a semi-circle behind him. Jason and Mark lowered Tyler to the ground, slowly sinking into fighting stances. Fire engulfed Jason's hands and Mark focused on the men nearest to him for his attack.

"I wouldn't try to fight if I were you." Greco warned, taking a step to the side. Mark hissed in frustration when he saw who was behind him. Ethan held Emma trapped in front of him, a gag in her mouth to keep her silent. His large hand was wrapped around her neck, sharp claws digging into her skin just above her jugular vein. "I would hate to see such a pretty girl get hurt in our fight." Greco said in a mocking voice.

186

Tears pricked Emma's eyes as she watched Mark and Jason slowly stand up, their faces void of expression. Despair spiraled through her at the thought that they were about to be captured because of her. In a desperate movement Emma jerked in Ethan's hold, trying to fight free. Ethan didn't even budge from her flailing. He tightened his grip on her neck, cutting off Emma's supply of air until she was gasping for breath. On her neck his nails felt like shards of glass digging into her skin. Suffocation made her hyper aware of the painful sensation, every single pinpoint of pain was magnified in her mind. If Emma had had any air in her body she would have whimpered. Emma felt something trickle down her neck and for a moment she thought it was a tear but with a sickening jolt she realized that it was blood she was feeling. One of Ethan's nails had pierced her skin.

"She's a feisty little one." Greco said, his expression amused. "Normally I would have fun breaking that wild spirit of hers but Drake wants her brought to him in one piece."

"Tell him to stop! She's suffocating!" Mark yelled. His expression was thunderous and Emma could see his hands shaking where they were clenched into fists by his side.

Greco glanced over his shoulder with a bored expression. "Ethan, we can't kill her yet. You know what our orders are."

Ethan kept his grip on Emma's neck for another moment. Emma thought she was going to pass out. Her head felt like it was going to explode and every cell of her body screamed for oxygen. Then his grip loosened and air seeped into her lungs. Emma gasped for breath, almost choking on the gag in her mouth. Emma continued dragging air into her body, feeling a deep sense of relief that she could breathe again.

"What do you want, Greco?" Mark growled.

Emma tried to catch Mark's eye so he could see how sorry she was but his gaze never wavered from Greco. His lips pulled back from his teeth in a silent snarl. The only thing keeping him from attacking was Emma.

Greco laughed. "I already have what I want." He told Mark. "This whole set up was just so I could get my hands on her. When the two of you first arrived I was a little worried she wasn't going to make it because she wasn't with you. But then she came sneaking up all on her own."

"Why do you want her?" Jason demanded.

"That's between Drake and the girl." Greco replied disinterestedly. "You were right to keep her hidden. As soon as Drake heard about her he wanted to see her for himself."

"We will do a better job at keeping her hidden next time." Mark growled.

"Unfortunately for you there won't be a next time." Greco drawled. "I'm tired of your boy guardian act. Now that I have Tyler and the girl I have no need for either of you." Greco motioned to two of his fighters. Fear burst through Emma as the two men leapt towards Mark and Jason. She screamed against the gag in her mouth, every ounce of fear she was feeling pouring out in her voice. When he heard her scream flames burst out all along Jason's arms, brighter than Emma had ever seen them. She felt the wave of heat hit her face and her skin tighten as the moisture was drawn out of it. All around them Greco's men stumbled back, blinking from the unexpected heat and light.

"Emma! Shield!" Jason yelled before releasing a streaming inferno directly at her. Emma quickly channeled her fear through the bracelet, praying that it would work. Greco dove out of the way as the flames engulfed Emma, sliding around her and torching Ethan instead. With a curse Ethan dove out of the way, beating himself to put out the flames that had caught on his clothes. Behind Emma the glass window shattered from the heat and the wooden frame around the window caught fire. Mark didn't wait for the flames to stop, he sprinted forward, feeling the flames sear his back for just a moment before he grabbed Emma and dove out the empty hole where the window had been.

Jason pulled Tyler up from the floor, still shooting flames at whoever tried to stand up as he and Tyler stumbled across the room towards the window. Within seconds the sparse amount of furniture was up in flames and smoke filled the air, making it impossible to breathe or see. The shadowy figures of Greco's men surrounded them in the smoke, just as blinded as Jason and Tyler were. Tyler stumbled and fell to the floor, gasping for air and too weak to move.

"Tyler!" Jason shouted over the roar of the flames. He tugged at Tyler's arm. "We have to go *now*! Get up!"

Tyler shook his head weakly. "No, no, no!" He yelled back weakly, coughing from the effort. "Hot, it's so hot. Can't breathe! Go, you go!"

Jason shook his head stubbornly. "I'm getting you out of here!" He yelled.

Jason reached down and grabbed Tyler, throwing him across his shoulders in a fireman carry. The fire had reached the ceiling and above them the roof beams groaned from the stress of the heat. The cabin wasn't going to last much longer. Jason stumbled over bodies of Greco's men who were passed out on the floor as he stumbled towards the window. He could see it just ahead of him, a small hole in a wall of flames. The flames around the window roared and expanded as the night breeze rushed in and fanned them to greater heights.

Through the thick smoke an arm swung through the air, hitting Jason in the chest with the force of a battering ram. Jason was knocked off his feet and he slammed onto his back on the floor. Tyler fell a few feet away from him and when Jason glanced over he didn't see Tyler moving. Jason tried to crawl over to him but Ethan jumped out of the smoke and grabbed him by the ankle. With a grunt Ethan dragged Jason towards him as Jason tried to scramble away.

"No, you don't." Ethan growled. Picking Jason up by the back of his clothes Ethan lifted Jason high into the air and slammed him down on the small table in the room. The table shattered beneath Jason, sparks flying into the air and flames whooshed out from underneath the tabletop.

Jason lay there gasping as pain filled every cell in his body. He could feel the anger growing inside of him, taking him over. He tried to fight it, tried to resist the darkness within him. The flames surrounding him roared at his pain, fueling the heat of his anger. Ethan appeared over him, canine's elongated and his appearance animalistic. With a large clawed hand Ethan reached down towards Jason.

"Don't touch me. You don't know what will happen." Jason warned him. Jason's voice was warped like the flames that were devouring the cabin. He was about to lose himself to the flames entirely and when that happened…

"You don't scare me weakling." Ethan snarled, grasping the front of Jason's coat and lifting Jason high into the air. With a roar Ethan slammed Jason into the cement floor. Jason's head cracked against the cement and pain burst through him again. In a daze he watched as Ethan straightened above him, lifting one booted foot to slam down on Jason's chest. Flames filled the edges of Jason's vision so all he could see was the look of gloating triumph on Ethan's face. Vaguely he heard Greco yell, "Ethan! Don't!" But then the flames took over.

Outside Emma crouched next to Mark who had collapsed on the ground. His back was seriously burned and his shirt was just a rag. Emma glanced back at the cabin that was going up in flames.

"Jason and Tyler are still in there!" Emma exclaimed. "We have to help them."

Mark coughed and drew in a raspy breath. "Jason will get them out." He grunted.

"But the cabin is going to collapse any moment!" Emma argued. "Why haven't they escaped yet?"

Mark pushed himself to his knees with a wince but when he looked back at the cabin a look of alarm crossed his face. He straightened up, any concern for his pain gone.

"Oh no." He whispered. "JASON, DON'T!" He roared.

"Mark, what's going on?" Emma demanded.

Mark dove on top of her as the cabin exploded into flame. Emma felt the wind get knocked out of her as the wave of heat hit them like a brick wall. The clearing lit up, everything illuminated by the giant bonfire the cabin had become.

"Jason!" Emma screamed. She struggled against Mark, trying to get free but he kept her pinned beneath him.

"No!" Mark shouted in her face. He gripped her face between his large hands, forcing her eyes to look into his. "Emma stop! Jason is gone, that's not him in there!"

The flames eased back after the initial burst but Emma could still feel the heat, even thirty feet away. Mark pushed himself up and pulled Emma to her feet.

"We have to leave, now!" Mark ordered, dragging her to the edge of the clearing.

"No!" Emma yelled at him, digging in her heels. "I'm not leaving without Jason!"

Mark whirled around to yell at her and Emma slapped him. His momentary shock loosened his grip just enough for Emma to pull herself free. She sprinted towards what was left of the cabin.

"Jason!" She screamed.

"Emma!" Mark yelled after her. "Don't! He's dangerous!"

Emma stumbled to a stop ten feet away from the cabin. The heat from the flames was intense but that wasn't what had stopped her. Through the remains of the window she saw the shape of a man moving through the flames.

"Jason!" Emma called out.

The figure paused, then walked towards the window. Emma gasped when they got closer. What she thought had been a man was a creature made entirely of fire. Everything it touched burst into flames. And the creature liked it. She could feel its enjoyment from where she stood. The figure beckoned her towards it, an evil smile spreading across its face. Emma felt a tear slide down her cheek, evaporating before it reached her chin.

"Jason?" Emma said.

The figure nodded its head.

Emma took a step closer and the creature smiled in delight.

"Emma!" Mark yelled. "Don't get any closer! It wants to kill you!"

The figure roared in anger and shot a ball of fire at Mark. Mark dove out of the way, grunting in pain as the ball of fire was extinguished in the dirt.

"Mark!" Emma yelled. Mark pushed himself to his feet with a wince and stumbled forward but without Emma's shield to dull the heat he couldn't get closer than twenty feet.

"Emma, come back here! He can't be helped!" Mark yelled, shielding his face with a thick arm.

"I'm not leaving him!" She yelled back. Emma turned back to the figure standing in the window. "Jason, I know you are still in there." She said to the creature. "You can control yourself, I know you can."

The creature shook its head in denial. Emma took another step towards the cabin and after hesitating the creature stepped closer to the window as well. She was only five feet away from the creature now, close enough to see it's eyes that glowed like two pieces of coal in a fire.

"Jason." Emma said softly, wincing when something crashed inside the cabin and the flames flared up again. "We need you. Come back."

The creature looked confused. It's head swayed back and forth as if it were battling two different urges. As Emma stared at the creature she briefly saw it's eyes flicker and become ice blue before turning back to burning coal.

Emma slowly stretched her hand out toward the creature like she would to a skittish animal. "It's okay." She crooned softly. "Just take my hand." Emma felt the tension of the moment, knew that she was risking being dragged into the cabin with the others, but she couldn't give up on Jason. Just when Emma thought there was no hope the creature reached it's hand out and touched it's fingers to hers.

Emma gasped as sensations and emotions crashed through her. Anger, so much anger, and darkness. She was drowning in it, overwhelmed by the burning within her. A burning that needed to be free, that needed everything else to burn too. The flames called to the anger, magnified it, drew it out, so strong she couldn't resist it, couldn't break free.

Then she saw the darkness, deep within the anger she saw the shadow that had been planted within the flames. Emma was buffeted by the anger and the flames but she struggled towards the shadow that she knew was the source of all the chaos. In her mind she reached towards that seed of darkness, her hand glowing with a light entirely different from the flames. With a touch the darkness disappeared, every hint of it gone from the flames. Emma felt a brief moment of satisfaction before exhaustion hit her like a train and everything went black.

The first thing Emma saw when she opened her eyes were the stars above the clearing. Pain pounded through her head like she had just had a spike driven into her brain. With a groan she brought a hand to her head. "What happened?"

Mark and Jason's faces appeared above hers. "Emma? Are you okay?" They both asked, speaking over each other.

"I think so." Emma said, squinting up at them. "My head hurts too much to think."

"Don't try to move yet, give your body time to adjust." Mark cautioned her.

Emma nodded carefully. Then she looked at Jason curiously.

"What happened to your clothes?"

Jason grinned ruefully and tugged Mark's jacket a little more snugly around his hips. "They burned off in the fire."

Emma nodded as she digested that piece of information. "Okay." She said simply. Emma looked at Mark. "Can we go home now?"

Mark chuckled. "Yes, we can go home."

Emma didn't speak the entire drive home as Mark drove her car, Jason wrapped in a blanket in the back seat. Mark drove to Jason's house first. He didn't trust leaving Emma alone quite yet. Once inside Mark settled her on the couch and gave her a glass of water. Emma took a small sip and then set it aside before stretching out on the couch.

"Emma." Mark said softly. "Are you okay?"

Emma shook her head. "No Mark, I'm not okay." She said quietly. "People died tonight, I saw them die. So no, I am not okay."

Mark reached out to stroke her hair, struggling to think of something to say.

"Mark." Jason called from the kitchen.

Mark froze, his fingers nearly grazing Emma's hair. With a sigh he pulled his hand back and got up to walk into the kitchen.

"What?" He murmured, glancing back into the room where Emma sat staring at the wall.

Jason's face was grim. "Loraine is gone."

Mark's gaze snapped back to Jason's, then he hurried over to the stairway to the basement.

"What do you mean, she's gone?" He snapped.

"I mean she is no longer here." Jason replied. "She must have escaped when we went up to the mountains."

"How?" Mark asked. "Her hands were securely tied, she can't use her powers without her hands."

Mark burst into the basement, looking around frantically. The chair Loraine had been sitting in was empty, the handcuffs they had used to hold her were open and draped over the back of the chair.

"I don't know." Jason said. "Maybe she had help, or maybe she's stronger than we thought."

"She tricked us." Mark muttered, staring at the empty chair.

"Do you think this whole thing was a set up?" Jason asked.

Mark turned and looked at him, his face sad. "All of this was for nothing."

Jason shook his head. "Not for nothing." He said. "Tyler told you something before we were captured. What was it?"

Mark rubbed his face with a hand. "He said that Emma needed to be protected, that she is a Forgeron."

Jason froze, his eyes wide in shock. "Impossible." He whispered.

Mark didn't say anything. He looked back at Emma's silhouette in the dark living room where she still hadn't moved.

"Do you know what this means?" A hint of fear tinted Jason's voice as he stared at Emma, too. "Do you know how many people will be after her if anyone finds out?"

"Then we don't let anyone find out." Mark replied.

"Do you think she knows?" Jason asked, looking at Mark.

Mark frowned. "We can't ask her tonight, she's in too much shock." He said. "I'm going to take her home with me, she can stay at my place tonight. She can't go home in this condition. When you've recovered go get the dirt bikes from the mountain."

"Why don't you just let her stay here?" Jason asked. "It may be better not to move her right now."

Mark shook his head. "Loraine knows how to get here now, I don't want to risk her coming back for Emma."

Jason glared at him but Mark's expression was unyielding. "Alright," Jason said grudgingly, "You're probably right. Keep her safe tonight."

Mark nodded once and went back upstairs to get Emma.

Early morning light illuminated the smoke curling up from the charred wreckage of the cabin. Loraine gingerly stepped through the blackened remains of the doorway and looked around. Ash swirled around her feet and up into the air, making her cough. Everything in the cabin was blackened and charred, ravaged by the fire. She nudged a black lump with her foot and it disintegrated into a pile of ash.

"How did this happen?" She muttered to herself.

She moved farther into the room, checking every charred lump she came across until she reached the back of the room where the stairs were. Turning her back to the stairs she surveyed the room again.

"Eight remains." She muttered to herself. "But there were nine people trapped in here. Where did the last one go?"

That was when she heard the scratching sound of something moving behind her. Slowly she turned, staring down into the darkness the steps led into. Harsh, labored breathing echoed off the walls as whatever it was began dragging itself up the steps. As the thing came into sight Loraine stumbled back, a gasp wrenching from her lips. Eyes wide she pressed the back of her hand to her mouth, fighting the urge to be sick.

From between melted and deformed lips the creature hissed,

"Emma Savage…willll…die."